LOVE STEALS THE SCENE

Other books by Carol Costa:

Labor of Love

LOVE STEALS
THE SCENE

•

Carol Costa

Published by Thomas Bouregy & Co., Inc.
160 Madison Avenue, New York, NY 10016

PRINTED IN THE UNITED STATES OF AMERICA
ON ACID-FREE PAPER
BY HADDON CRAFTSMEN, BLOOMSBURG, PENNSYLVANIA

For the Costa kids: Angela Ann, Joseph Robert,
and Michael Riley

Chapter One

"**A** toast to our guest of honor," Hilary shouted, raising her champagne glass in the air and gently pushing Linda into the center of the room. "May Hollywood love her as much as we do!"

Linda smiled as the party guests sipped their champagne and added their own good wishes to Hilary's. "Thank you," Linda said. "I'm overwhelmed by all of this attention, but I'll do my best to live up to your expectations."

"Just remember me when it's time to cast the movie," a female voice called out.

Her remark was followed by several others of similar intent. "I guess I'll have to add a lot of characters to this script," Linda replied with a dazzling smile.

"Okay," Hilary shouted again. "Auditions are over. The buffet table is set up in the conference room."

A few people cheered, and everyone began to make their way towards the conference room where the catering staff waited to serve them.

Linda turned to Hilary, her agent and friend. "This is wonderful. How did you organize this party so quickly?"

"Are you kidding? Mention free food, and the whole theater community comes to your door. I'll bet there are people here who don't even know you."

Linda laughed. "You're right, but I love them all for showing up to support me."

"Does that include me?" Rick Ralston bent down to kiss Linda on the cheek.

"I think I hear the caterer calling," Hilary said, making a hasty departure.

Linda looked up into the dark, deep set eyes of her former boyfriend. Rick projected the image of a perfect romantic leading man. On stage he was a skilled actor capable of mesmerizing an audience, in person he was even more dangerous.

"Hello, Rick," Linda said, inching away from the arm he had dropped over her shoulder.

"I wasn't sure I'd be welcome at your party, but I couldn't let you leave New York without at least trying to talk to you."

"Oh, really?" Linda replied in an icy tone. "It seems you've survived quite well over the past few weeks without speaking to me."

"Linda, please." Rick gave her one of his lingering looks, the kind that used to melt down her resistance like ice cream on a hot summer day. "Give me a chance to explain."

"I think I did that," Linda answered in the same cool tone. "When I caught you with Susan, and then again with Heather, and again with . . ."

"Stop," Rick protested. "I know I hurt you, and I don't deserve another chance. I acted like an idiot, but without you I *am* an idiot, floundering around like a fish out of water."

"You learn your lines well, Rick, and still deliver them with all the charm and cunning of the devil himself."

"Okay, so you're not going to fall into my arms again," he said softly. "But can't we be friends?"

"I don't know," Linda said honestly. "I'll think about it while I'm away."

Before Rick could enter another plea, Linda hurried off to mingle with the other guests. Rick watched her from across the room for a moment or two, but he wasn't alone for long. The next time Linda glanced in his direction he was being comforted by three young actresses.

"Hey, Linda," a gentle voice whispered in her ear. "Forget that bum, and tell me about your deal."

"Freddie!" Linda threw her arms around the rotund off-Broadway producer who had staged her first play. "I didn't see you come in."

"You were too busy looking at the desk clerk from Heartbreak Hotel."

Linda hugged him again. "I'm so glad to see you. Hilary said you were doing a show in Connecticut. I didn't think you'd be here."

"Sweetie, when I heard the news, I told my cast to take the night off. I wouldn't miss this party for the world. So tell me everything."

"Well," Linda paused for the proper dramatic effect, then broke into a huge grin. "Last week, Frank Dancer was in New York, and he just happened to catch a performance of *The Last Laugh*. The next day, he tracked Hilary down and made an offer for the film rights."

"And you get to write the script."

"Sort of . . . Dancer wants me to collaborate with an experienced screenwriter, a man named John Harper."

"John Harper. Well, I'm impressed. He's what they call an 'A-list' writer."

"I leave for California tomorrow afternoon."

"Knowing Hilary, that means you've already banked a sizable advance."

"It's not bad," Linda admitted. "Oh, Freddie, if it weren't for you . . ."

"Sweetie, you have the talent. All I did was cash in on it."

"Without you, I'd still be waiting tables," Linda insisted. "Who talked Hilary Marshall into coming to see that first production?"

"I did. Talent like yours needs a high roller like Hilary.

And now it's paid off for both of you. Honestly, Linda, I couldn't be happier if you were my own daughter."

This brought tears to Linda's soft brown eyes, but they were soon erased by laughter as Freddie began relating some of the hilarious experiences from his latest production.

The next time Linda looked across the room, Rick Ralston was gone. It wasn't like him to give up so easily, but perhaps he was waiting to see if her success was going to last before he used all his firepower on her.

Frank Dancer's movie offer was the beginning of a dream come true for Linda, but there could be many long, restless nights ahead before the dream became a reality.

Chapter Two

Two days later, Linda pushed through a glass door with "Dancer Productions" written in bold black letters on it. A receptionist looked up from the newspaper she was reading and acknowledged Linda with a courteous smile.

"I'm Linda Lucas. I have a ten-thirty appointment with Mr. Dancer."

"Oh, yes." The girl's smile grew warmer. "I spoke to you on the phone last week. I'm Julie."

"Hi, Julie."

"Just have a seat. Mr. Dancer will be with you in a few minutes."

Linda settled herself in one of the sleek leather and chrome chairs placed in a semicircle in front of an enormous window that overlooked Beverly Hills. Julie went back to her newspaper as Linda gazed out the window at the view still partially obscured by the morning smog.

I'm really here, Linda thought, *I'm really on my way . . .*

Her thoughts were interrupted by the noisy entrance of a young man clad in shorts, a partially buttoned Hawaiian shirt, and a pair of dirty, worn-out tennis shoes. Linda watched as the unkempt intruder lifted the receptionist off her chair and gave her an enthusiastic hug.

"Scott," Julie screamed, obviously delighted by his embrace. "How wonderful to see you."

5

He must be her boyfriend, Linda decided with a tolerant smile and a nod in their direction.

Scott suddenly turned his attention to Linda. "Hi, how are you?" he asked.

"Fine, thank you," Linda answered politely.

"I'm Scott Richards." With a few quick strides, he was at Linda's side, extending his hand to her.

"Nice to meet you," Linda said, wondering why he had left his girlfriend to talk to her. She took his hand and found herself being pulled from the chair to her feet.

"You're a small one." Scott grinned. "But just as pretty as your picture."

Linda stared up at his unshaven face, ruggedly handsome and tanned to perfection. His smile was disarming, and his eyes were so blue that they made Linda think of a peaceful lake.

"Pardon me?" Linda asked, pulling her hand away from the impulsive stranger.

Julie hurried over to them. "I'm sorry, Miss Lucas. Someone should have warned you about Scott."

Linda was confused. They were both acting like she should know who this brash young man was. But before she could say anything else, Scott grabbed her hand again and pulled her towards Mr. Dancer's inner office.

Scott barged right through the door with Linda stumbling along behind him. "Okay, Frank, we've been waiting long enough. Let's get this meeting started."

Linda recognized Frank Dancer from the brief meeting they'd had in New York. The producer rose from his seat behind a huge, highly polished mahogany desk.

"Linda, sorry to keep you waiting. Good to see you again." Dancer reached out to shake Linda's hand, which she once again had to pull from Scott's strong grip. "I see you've already met your co-writer."

The bewilderment that made Linda's eyes appear even larger caused Dancer to begin a quick, apologetic explanation. "Oh, sorry, doll, I forgot to tell you. John Harper was committed to another project, so Scott here will be working with you on the screenplay."

"I see," Linda managed to stammer. "Oh . . . um . . . I left my things in the reception area."

She wanted an excuse to retreat. Her mind was refusing to accept what Dancer had just told her. This man, who looked like he had just washed up on the beach, was her co-writer.

"Julie," Dancer called out through the open door. "Bring Linda's things in here." Then he turned to Linda again. "Please, sit down. Would you like some coffee?"

"No, thanks," Linda replied with a weak smile.

Scott had already plopped himself into one of the two chairs facing Dancer's desk. He was perfectly at ease, running a casual hand through his sun-bleached blond hair and grinning at Linda's pained expression.

"Hey, relax," Scott told her in a pleasant tone. "I'm really not a bad guy once you get to know me. And please don't let the fact that I have no talent, and got this assignment because Frank is married to my big sister, worry you. We'll get through this just fine."

Julie handed Linda her purse and briefcase, and Linda sat down gingerly on the other chair while Scott and Dancer laughed heartily over Scott's last remark.

This was all a joke to them. Hilary had warned her that these Hollywood people were a bunch of crazies.

"Now seriously, Linda," Dancer said, sitting down behind the desk again. "Despite the fact that Scott is my brother-in-law, he does have some talent. We just have to figure out what it is."

This time, Linda laughed along with the two men, but wild thoughts were racing through her mind. This was her big break, the one she had worked and planned for all these years.

This was the important meeting she had prepared for so carefully. Before leaving New York, she had spent days shopping for the simple but expensive suit she was wearing.

It was just the right shade of blue to compliment her un-blemished olive complexion and jet black hair.

Linda raised her hand to feel the shortness of her chic new hairstyle and then looked down at the stylish white pumps that made her legs appear longer and thinner.

All the pains she had taken to look just right for this meeting, only to find herself in a plush Beverly Hills office with a pair of comedians bantering like they were on the vaudeville circuit.

"Look," Linda finally said, directing a serious gaze at Frank Dancer and then at Scott. "This is all very amusing, but I am anxious to discuss your plans for my play. I've been thinking about the type of films your company usually produces, and I'm not sure how my script will fit in with your other projects."

"For such a tiny girl," Scott remarked, totally ignoring her request for seriousness, "you've got fabulous legs. Are you a swimmer?"

"No, I'm not. In fact, I find the beach hot and boring." Linda was upset, and tired of his attempts to flatter her.

Undaunted, Scott grinned at her. "That's only because you've never been on my beach."

"Okay, Scott, enough," Dancer said quickly. "This is a business meeting and, as usual, you look awful. You've got Linda convinced that you're a bum."

"I am a bum," Scott admitted cheerfully. "So why try and hide it?"

"You're also a good screenwriter, which is why I've as-signed you to work with Linda." At last Dancer was taking charge of the meeting, and Linda immediately felt better. He turned to her and smiled. "To answer your question about the play, I bought the film rights and got you out here to work on the script because I feel it's time my com-pany broke out of the rut it's in. Not that thrillers haven't been very lucrative—they have—but we don't want to be stuck with that image forever. My latest release, which pre-mieres this week, is a musical. And by the way, I'm ex-pecting both of you to attend the premiere and the party afterwards. Anyway, Miss Lucas, your play fits right in with my future plans to produce more comedies and films for a family audience."

Linda nodded and relaxed a little more. She sat back in her chair and crossed her shapely legs. Scott smiled his approval in a way that annoyed her even more than his earlier remarks.

Why doesn't he at least button his shirt? she asked herself. Then, noticing the broadness of his shoulders and chest, she decided that the shirt was probably too small to close around him.

Her next thought was that Scott had a lot of nerve referring to her as small or tiny, since he wasn't very tall himself—five foot seven at the most. He probably had a hard time finding women who didn't tower over him. Of course, his ego seemed large enough for an Amazon woman.

"Miss Lucas? . . . Linda?" Frank Dancer's voice rose slightly as he attempted to regain Linda's attention.

Linda suddenly realized that she had been ignoring Dancer and staring openly at Scott. "I'm sorry," Linda said, as Scott gave her another of his perfect smiles. Linda couldn't help noticing the way his grin made the corners of his eyes crinkle like they had to keep the mirth from spilling out of blue pools. Turning back to Dancer, Linda focused her gaze on the producer's balding head and repeated her apology. "I'm sorry, what were you saying?"

"Just that I think your play is delightful, and so does everyone on my staff who's read it," Dancer replied.

"Thank you. And I want you to know how much I appreciate the opportunity to work on the screenplay. I'll do the very best job I can for you."

"Yes, I'm sure you will, but as we discussed in New York, since your experience is limited to live theater, you will need some guidance to take the story from the stage to the screen. That, of course, is where Scott comes in."

Linda nodded and turned towards Scott, daring to meet

his eyes again. "I suppose you have some ideas about the script?" she asked.

"No, actually, I haven't even read it yet."

"Scott," Dancer said, with annoyance in his voice, "I gave you a copy last week."

Scott grinned sheepishly. "I know, but I can't find it. You know what a mess my place is always in. Anyway, I'll bet Linda has another I can read right in that neat little brief-case of hers."

"As a matter of fact, I do," Linda told him as she deftly snapped open the briefcase and produced a bound copy of the play script.

"Thanks, honey. I promise not to lose this one."

"Now listen, Scott," Dancer warned. "I want this script completed by the end of next month. I'm already casting for the film."

"Sure, Frank," Scott replied, looking only at Linda. "We'll get it done on time."

"Fine," the producer agreed. "You two set up your own work schedule. You can use one of my offices, if you like."

"Oh, that would be great," Linda said.

Scott shook his blond curls and made a face. "Too many distractions in the city," he complained. "It will be better to work at my house. I've got everything we need right there, including an ocean." He stood up and held out a hand to Linda. "Come on. I'll take you there right now. You can drive and I'll read the script on the way."

"Are you serious?" Linda asked, feeling off balance again.

"Sure. What's wrong? Don't you know how to drive?"

"Of course I do."

"Good, then let's go. See you, Frank."

Mr. Dancer was nodding his approval of Scott's sugges-tion, so Linda felt obliged to go along with it.

"Okay," she agreed hesitantly. "I guess that will be all right."

Scott took her arm and began to usher her out of the

office. Linda looked back at Dancer, but he just waved and smiled.

"Don't forget," Dancer called after them. "I want both of you at the premiere next Saturday."

Chapter Three

Linda let Scott lead her out of the building and across the parking lot to his car. He had kept up a constant flow of chatter during their trek to the car, and greeted everyone they met in the hallways and elevator. Linda had remained silent, mostly because she didn't know what to do or say about the situation she was in.

"Here we are," he announced, opening the driver's side door of an older but very nice white Cadillac convertible. "Just throw your things in the back."

"Nice car," Linda commented, breaking her silence. "I was sure you'd be driving a Volkswagen Beetle."

"I would be," Scott agreed cheerfully. "But my sister forced me to take this one. She was very attached to it, and when Frank bought her a new car, she wanted to keep this one in the family."

Scott held the door as Linda slid behind the wheel, and then he handed her a set of car keys. Linda started the car, adjusted the seats and mirrors to her liking, and in a few minutes, under Scott's direction, she was driving on a freeway heading towards the ocean.

The rest of the morning smog had burned off and it was a lovely, warm day. The Cadillac handled easily and the freeway traffic was moving smoothly, so Linda decided to push the disappointment and apprehension from her mind and just enjoy the sunshine and the ride. Back in New York, they were still wearing overcoats. Scott was finally silent as he read through the pages of her script.

The Last Laugh was about four couples who found romance during the famous World Series of 1960 between the New York Yankees and the Pittsburgh Pirates.

Most of the stage version took place in a neighborhood restaurant where the guys argued and bet on the World Series and the girls thought of ways to attract their attention. One of the girls had a Pirates hat and claimed that it had the power to influence the outcome of the games.

A lot of the other humor in the play revolved around the fact that all of the characters liked to play practical jokes on one another. It had turned into a contest between the guys and girls to see who could set up the best ruse.

The so-called lucky hat and the practical jokes both allowed Linda to develop very humorous dialogue and scenes.

Scott seemed to be enjoying the script, and was even laughing out loud. Linda felt immensely relieved. Perhaps they would be able to establish a good working relationship despite their obvious differences.

"Take the next exit," Scott said, looking up from the script for a moment. "Then turn right at the light and follow the road. It leads right to my house."

Linda soon found herself driving alongside the Pacific Ocean. It was a beautiful sight, especially for a girl who had spent most of the last six years confined to the concrete world of New York City. Of course she had an ocean on her side of the country too, but she rarely ventured out to enjoy it.

Thirty minutes later, they arrived at Scott's beach house. Access to the house was from the back, and Scott had her pull the car into a carport. The roof of the carport was actually the first floor of a house that rested on huge rough timbers rising out of the sand.

Beyond the pillars, just a few hundred yards away, Linda could see the white-capped waves breaking on the shore.

The air was cool and crisp. She got out of the car and took a deep breath, filling her lungs with the fresh scent of sea and sand.

The house was constructed of irregular gray stone and dark wood. Off to the left was a wooden staircase leading up to the door.

"I'll finish this later," Scott said indicating the script he had now tucked under his arm. "It's very good. I think Frank made a wise decision."

"Thank you." The compliment relaxed Linda a little more, but she was still feeling very uncomfortable.

Scott came around to take the car keys from her hand. The ground alongside the car was soft and sandy. As Linda stepped toward the house in her high-heeled shoes, she sank into the sand and was suddenly pitched forward.

Scott tried to catch her, but the force of her unexpected fall caused him to stumble backwards. The script went sailing through the air as they went down together in a heap. Linda landed on top of Scott with her face buried against his bare chest and his strong arms wrapped around her.

Stunned by the fall, neither of them moved for a few seconds, then Scott began to laugh. Linda could feel the vibration of his chest against her cheek, and she too began to laugh.

The two lay entangled in the sand as the roar of the ocean mingled with the sound of their laughter. Despite the awkwardness of her position, Linda felt free of tension for the first time in days.

"I'm sorry," Linda finally managed to say. "My shoes just sank right in, and I toppled over."

"For such a little girl," Scott answered, still holding onto her, "You don't have any trouble knocking a guy off his feet."

His words made Linda suddenly aware of her body pressed against his, and she struggled to free herself from his arms. Scott obliged by loosening his hold on her and letting her gently slide off of him. Linda sat up quickly and concentrated on removing her shoes.

"I'm so embarrassed," Linda mumbled, dumping sand from her shoes.

Scott laughed again. "Don't be. I loved it." He scrambled to his feet and offered her his hand. Linda felt hot and flushed as she allowed him to help her up.

Now she could feel the sun-baked sand burning through her hose, and she moved quickly to the stairs. Scott shook his head, again amused by her. He took the stairs two at a time and opened the door for them.

The house was dark compared to the brightness of the sun outside, and Linda took off her sunglasses and waited for her eyes to adjust to the dimness.

"Make yourself at home," Scott called out as he went back outside to retrieve the script and Linda's briefcase and purse from the car.

Linda turned around in a slow circle, cooling her feet on the smooth tile floor. The room was very large, stretching across the entire width of the house. At the ocean side was a wall of windows from floor to ceiling that were covered by roll-up bamboo shades. In the center of the far wall was a massive stone fireplace with the ashes of its last fire still in the hearth.

As Scott had mentioned in Dancer's office, the place was a mess. There was a lot of furniture. Casual, comfortable-looking sofas and chairs with assorted tables and lamps were spread out across the room, with no real pattern or style. A heavy antique desk was placed near the wall opposite the fireplace, and this was obviously Scott's work area. A computer, scanner, and printer occupied the top of the desk, but these were obscured by the clutter of papers, scripts, and books which overflowed to the rest of the room and mixed in with magazines, newspapers, and an endless assortment of photographs and knickknacks.

Scott returned and flashed Linda a friendly smile.

"You were right," she said wryly. "This place is a mess."

"Feel free to clean up if it will make you more comfortable," he replied easily. "Come on. I'll show you the rest of the house."

Linda followed Scott through a doorway behind them that led to a small bright dinette area and galley-type kitchen. There was a pass-through window from the kitchen into the living room. In the dinette area, there was a round table and two chairs set in an alcove of three unshaded windows.

"No dirty dishes," Linda remarked. She was surprised by the neatness of the kitchen compared to the living room.

"Paper plates and very little cooking." Scott nodded towards the microwave oven on the counter between the sink and the refrigerator.

On the other side of the kitchen was the area of the house over the carport, and a square hallway led to two large bedrooms, each with its own full bath and large walk-in closet.

"This is the guest room," Scott told her, after closing the door on the untidiness of his own sleeping quarters and leading her across the hall to the other room. "How do you like it?"

"It's lovely," Linda said. And it was. A large four-poster bed was covered with a beautiful handmade quilt of bright calico squares. A tall dresser stood against one wall, and next to it was a reading area with an armchair, table, and lamp. On the other side of the room, long windows afforded a view of the beach and ocean. In front of the windows was a writing desk and chair.

"It's all yours," Scott said.

"What did you say?" Linda asked, although she knew full well what he was suggesting.

"You can use this one," Scott repeated with a casual air.

"No. I don't think so," Linda replied firmly.

"Why not?"

"I think that's obvious."

"Oh, I get it." He grinned playfully, with wide innocent eyes. "You're afraid you won't be able to keep your hands off me."

"I'm not even going to dignify that remark with a response." Linda hurried out of the lovely room and retreated through the kitchen to the living room.

"Hey, honey, don't get mad," Scott said as he followed her. "I'm just trying to get you to lighten up. Life's too short to take it so seriously."

Linda spun around to face him with fire in her eyes. "Look, Mr. Richards, from the moment we met, you've done nothing but clown around," she shouted. "This movie means everything to me. It's what I've worked towards all my life. It's my chance at the gold ring, so I'm going back to Frank Dancer right now to ask him to assign someone else to work with me. Someone who will take it as seriously as I do."

Chapter Four

It wasn't until Linda had gathered her things and stormed out of the house that she realized she couldn't go anywhere. It was Scott's car, and he had the keys.

Still fuming, she looked up and down the beach. The closest house was about a hundred yards away. She would just have to go there and see if they would be kind enough to let her use their telephone. Or perhaps she could pay them to take her back to town.

Linda trudged through the sand, carrying her shoes and briefcase, with her purse slung over her shoulder. She stopped and removed her hose so she could walk along the edge of the water where the ground was smoother. The sand was wet and cold between her toes.

It didn't take Scott long to catch up and fall into step beside her. She decided to ignore him. She hiked her skirt up above her knees in order to take longer strides.

After they had walked in silence for a few yards, Scott spoke to her. "I hope you're not headed for that house over there." Linda didn't answer. "Because the people who live there are retired comedians, and I know you hate funny stuff." She still remained silent. "They were once known as the Crazy Cavanaughs, and they have no trouble living up to the name."

"Shut up!" Linda yelled. She abandoned the water's edge

and moved up the sandy slope towards the Cavanaughs' house.

"Okay," Scott agreed, falling silent for a few paces.

Linda followed a flower-lined path to a few steps that led to a patio. An older gentleman was sitting in a deck chair under an umbrella, reading a book.

"Excuse me," Linda called from the edge of the patio.

The man continued to read without looking up. "You'll have to talk louder," Scott told her. "He's deaf as a stone."

Linda tried the iron gate and it swung open. The patio stones were hot and rough as she limped towards the man in the deck chair. "Excuse me, sir," she shouted.

The man looked up at Linda. "Who are you?"

"I'm sorry to disturb you, but I was wondering if I could use your telephone?"

"Sure, but it will cost you."

"I'll be glad to pay for the call."

"How much?"

"Excuse me?"

"How much are you willing to pay? Phones don't grow on trees, you know." Then he saw Scott standing at the edge of the patio watching them. "Hey, Scott, you know this tomato?"

"Yes, sir. She's a writer from New York."

"New York," he yelled. "Forget it, girlie. You're not calling New York on my bill."

"I'm not going to call New York," Linda explained. "I just want to call a cab so I can get back to Beverly Hills."

"Fat chance," he told her. "Cabs don't come all the way out here to pick up fares. You need a ride, ask Scott. He's got a car."

"I don't want a ride from him," Linda said evenly.

"Why not?"

"Look, mister, it's a long story," Linda pleaded. "Can I just use your phone, please?"

"I like long stories," the older man said. "Have a seat and tell me about it. I got all day."

"Well, I don't," Linda said. "Excuse me for bothering you."

She turned and started to walk away, but the man jumped to his feet and grabbed her arm. "Did Scott take you to his house and make a pass at you?"

"Not exactly," Linda replied.

"Well, then, he's dumber than I thought he was." He let go of Linda and rushed over to confront Scott. "What's wrong with you, Scott? Pretty girls like this don't grow on trees, you know."

"I know, Charlie."

"Well, then don't just stand there. Make your move, man!"

"I would, but this girl is really tough. She's already knocked me down once today."

Charlie turned around and looked at Linda. "That little girl knocked you down?"

"Yes, sir."

Charlie thought that was very amusing. He began to laugh and slap his knees in merriment. "Well, that's the kind of girl you should marry. Any time you get too big for your britches, she knocks you down to size. I'll marry her myself."

"Mind your manners, Charlie. I'm not dressed for company, so don't make me come out there." The new voice came from inside the house. Linda turned and saw an elderly woman standing at an open window. She was dressed in a bathrobe with her hair in huge curlers.

"Oh, oh," Charlie said. "Watch out. LaVerne's transmitting from Mars again. Those metal doodads on her head are electronic pulsators."

Scott laughed and waved at LaVerne. "Hi, beautiful. This is Linda Lucas, a writer from New York."

"I heard. Nice to meet you, Linda. Don't mind my husband. He's harmless. Would you like a cold drink?"

"No, thank you. I have to be going." Linda pushed past Charlie and Scott, heading towards the beach and the next house down the way.

"Don't just stand there, Scott." Charlie pushed Scott towards the open gate. "She's getting away. Go after her."

Scott bounded down the steps and caught up with Linda again. "Hey, wait up, Linda."

"Was he right about the cabs not coming out here?" Linda asked quietly.

"Look, you don't need a cab. If you want to go back to town, I'll drive you."

"Fine. Let's go." Linda started walking back towards Scott's house.

"After lunch."

"Lunch?"

"Yeah, I hate to argue on an empty stomach, especially when I'm wrong."

"Is that an apology?" Linda asked, looking him straight in the eyes.

"Yes, it is," Scott said with a serious look. "I'm sorry, honest. I didn't mean to upset you, and I don't want you to get another writer for the project. I think you're very talented, and I was really looking forward to working with you. So how about giving me another chance?"

Linda stared into the blueness of his eyes. They seemed to shine with sincerity. Once again she felt confused by his ability to be both irritating and appealing. "Oh, you know darn well your brother-in-law would probably tell me to get lost if I asked for another writer."

"I doubt that, but give me another chance anyway."

Linda shrugged and managed a small smile. "Okay," she agreed. "What's for lunch? I'm starving."

"Follow me," Scott instructed. "And bring the script, I want to read some more."

Back at the house, Scott went into the kitchen and Linda looked around the living room for a place to sit. Finally, she pushed a pile of newspapers onto the floor and threw herself into a chair. Besides being hungry, she was tired and thirsty and regretted refusing Laverne's offer of a cold drink. She also knew that she must look a mess from trudging up and down the beach.

Scott stuck his head through the pass-through window and smiled at her. "For the record, when I suggested you stay here, I wasn't trying to proposition you. We don't have a lot of time to get this script ready, and that means long hours of hard work."

"I don't see why we can't work at Mr. Dancer's office like he suggested."

"Because we'd never get it finished in time. Trust me on this. I need total peace and quiet to work well. That's why I live way out here without a telephone."

"No telephone?" Linda was appalled. "How can you live here without a telephone?"

"It's easy. Try it for a week and you'll be hooked."

"I'll think about it," she conceded, too tired to argue any longer. "Do you have anything to drink?"

"That I do have, although the selections are limited."

"Anything cold will be fine," Linda replied.

"Okay. Tea or lemonade?"

"Lemonade, please."

A few seconds later, he stood in front of her with a frosty glass of lemonade. She took it and drank down half of it while he stood with his hands on his hips, watching her. Linda looked up at him and suddenly found herself remembering how strong his body had felt against hers.

"I thought you were fixing us lunch," she said sternly.

"Right. I hope you like quiche." He turned and went back to the kitchen, then stuck his head through the pass-through window again. "And one more thing," he said.

"What's that?"

"I'm very attracted to you. As Charlie said, pretty girls like you don't grow on trees, but I don't force myself on any woman. Frankly, I don't have to, they chase after me. That's another reason I live way out here. It keeps the girls at a safe distance."

"Your ego is unbelievable," Linda told him. She rose from the chair and walked towards the kitchen with her now-empty glass. "Excuse me," she said as she passed by him. "I'd like to freshen up."

"Sure, you know the way."

As Linda went into the hallway, Scott opened the freezer and began rummaging around inside of it. By the time she returned with a fresh-scrubbed face, the microwave was signaling that their lunch was ready.

Chapter Five

"**L**et's eat on the sundeck," Scott suggested. Linda followed him into the hallway again. "Open that door," he instructed, motioning to a door that Linda had assumed was a closet. The door opened onto a narrow staircase. "Go on up," Scott continued. "There's a sliding door at the top. The latch is on the right."

Linda climbed the dark, narrow staircase while Scott waited at the bottom holding a tray laden with their lunch. Linda found the latch and slid the door open, flooding the stairway with the light of the afternoon sun.

The deck looked out at the beach on one end and the distant city on the other. The effect was breathtaking.

The floor and the waist-high railing that surrounded the deck were redwood. There were heavy metal chairs with bright flowered cushions around a round metal table with a yellow umbrella rising from its center. Scott put the tray on the table and they sat down to eat.

Lunch consisted of quiche, fresh strawberries, and watermelon. They ate in silence for a few moments, then Scott sat back and looked at her appraisingly. "I'm not your type, huh?" he asked.

"That's right," Linda answered truthfully.

"I know. You like the smooth debonair guys like Rick Ralston. Are you still with him?"

Linda managed to swallow a bite of food without choking. "No," she replied curtly.

"Good."

Linda concentrated on her food. The mention of Rick Ralston had triggered her anger again. How did Scott know about Rick, and how did he have the gall to throw out his flippant remarks and ask questions that intruded on the personal areas of her life?

"You really were hungry," Scott commented. The blue pools of his eyes, filled with amusement, danced over her. Even when Scott's voice was silent, his eyes continued to speak to her.

"How did you manage the quiche?" she asked. "I thought you didn't cook."

"I don't. Carla made the quiche. She loves to cook, and delivers a carload of delicacies to my door every week or so."

"Carla?"

"My sister. You know, the one who makes Frank Dancer give me writing assignments."

"Right."

"So, what do you think of the beach house?"

"It's very nice. How long have you lived here?"

"A few years. My dad had it built a long time ago. When Carla and I were kids we spent all our summers here with my mom. After my mom died, Carla wanted to sell it, but I threw a tantrum, so she signed her half over to me. After she married Frank, I moved out here."

"Don't you get lonely?"

"Nope. I love the ocean, and I hate the city. I was born to be a bum."

"But you work. Writing is work."

"It can be. Fortunately, my parents left me enough money to live like this the rest of my life. I only write what I want, when I want."

Linda was annoyed. "I see," she replied.

"No, you don't," Scott said matter-of-factly. "You thoroughly disapprove of me and my lifestyle. You're a no-nonsense hard worker, and you think everyone should be that way."

Linda had to admit his assessment of her was right. An involuntary smile turned up the corners of her mouth. "Earlier you claimed you wanted to work with me and my script. Why?"

"I told you. I think you're very talented."

"But you haven't even read the whole play," Linda protested.

"I didn't need to read it. I'm familiar with your work." Now he had Linda's full attention, so he continued. "About a month ago, I spent some time in New York for a friend's wedding, and I saw one of your plays. It was a workshop production."

"Which one?"

"I don't remember the title of the play, but it was about a man with a camera that turned ugly people and things into beautiful pictures."

"*The Magic Camera.*"

"That was it. Anyway, I was very impressed by the warmth and humor of your characters. I always wished I could create people like that."

"Thank you, but the play didn't do as well as I hoped."

"Didn't you enjoy writing it?"

"Yes, of course I did."

"Then it was worthwhile."

Linda shrugged and smiled. "I guess I haven't looked at my writing that way for a long time."

The food and the warmth of the sun were very relaxing. Linda stretched and yawned.

"You're not going to fall asleep on me, are you?" Scott teased. "I know I'm no Rick Ralston, but I didn't think I was that boring."

The mention of Rick's name snapped Linda to attention again. Little prickles of irritation danced down her spine. "How do you know about Rick Ralston?" she asked pointedly.

Scott leaned back in his chair and took a sip of his drink. "After I saw your play, I wanted to meet you. I went backstage, but I was told you had already left with your boyfriend. The girl who supplied me with all the details was a blond actress. She played the part of Angelica in your play. I really love that name."

Linda instantly knew who Scott was referring to. Her real name was Marianne, another girl who Rick had romanced behind Linda's back. Linda got up quickly and walked over to the railing to look out at the ocean.

Seeing Rick at the party the other night had stirred up a lot of the old emotions. It wasn't that she was still in love with Rick, Linda thought, as she watched the water cover the sand and then recede to make way for the next bubbling wave. No, the love had slowly died, leaving only a sense of loss and failure. And now, like the sandy shore below her, Linda waited for love to roar in and touch her life again.

Scott walked over and stood behind her. Although he didn't touch her, Linda was very aware of his closeness. Thoughts of Rick and his betrayal of her made Linda feel small and vulnerable. It would be so easy to seek comfort in the arms of another man, and if she were to turn around at this moment, she felt certain that Scott Richards would be willing to take her in his strong arms and . . .

"I'd like to get back to town," Linda said suddenly. "Can we go now?"

Scott moved alongside of her. "Only if you promise to come back tomorrow." His tone was gentle, soft, and teasing, as if he could read her thoughts.

"Bright and early," Linda agreed, giving him a defiant smile.

Within a few minutes, they were back in the car speeding back toward the city. Scott decided to drive, so Linda sat in the passenger's seat and enjoyed the scenery.

The noise of the wind in the open car made it difficult to speak, so the ride to Linda's hotel contained very little conversation.

As they drove, Scott seemed to slip into his own thoughts, and Linda had the opportunity to study him unnoticed. Her eyes moved from the large strong hands effortlessly guiding the car to the tanned muscular arms, up to the handsome, still unshaven face. A pair of sunglasses now concealed the blue of his eyes that had such a disarming effect on her.

For a moment, Linda stared at the full, nicely shaped mouth and wondered what it would be like to feel his lips against her own. Would his kiss match the strength of the body and arms she had accidently tumbled into? Her gaze continued down to the impressive power of his perfectly browned legs, and then abruptly she looked away.

Her thoughts, she told herself, were as crazy as the man who sat beside her and as wild as the comments of Scott's old neighbor, Charlie. She was a city girl and she wanted a man who was a successful, well-dressed city dweller, not an irresponsible beach bum.

It was after 3:00 when Scott dropped Linda off at the hotel. They agreed that Linda would be at the beach house by 8:00 the following morning.

Linda went directly to her hotel room and, after showering and slipping into her favorite shorts and shirt, called the front desk and arranged for the rental car she would need to drive to the beach each day. All her accommodations, including the car, were being paid for by Dancer Productions.

After years of struggling to earn a living, the luxury of not having to worry about extra unexpected expenses was a pleasant change. All she had to worry about now was whether she would be able to work with Scott Richards.

Could this mismatched pair turn out a good screenplay? Linda fervently hoped their collaboration would work. More than anything, she wanted to be a success. Only then could she return to New York and flaunt her glorious achievements in Rick Ralston's lying, cheating face.

Chapter Six

The next morning, Linda dressed comfortably in a pair of blue jeans and a loose-fitting blouse. She slipped her bare feet into a pair of sandals. Today she would be prepared for the surroundings she was expected to work in.

Her rental car, a conservative Ford sedan, was waiting at the front door of the hotel. Linda had already studied the map she picked up at breakfast to make sure she could find her way back to the beach house.

Linda loaded her belongings into the car and sped off towards the beach. A few minutes later, she was trapped in freeway traffic.

Despite years of driving on the congested streets of New York City, Linda was not prepared for California's freeways during rush hour. It was very much like the bumper cars at Coney Island Amusement Park, with everyone fearlessly trying to get in front of everyone else in a race to their respective destinations.

By the time Linda arrived at the beach house, it was after ten and she was a wreck. Scott was probably wondering what had happened to her, she thought, as she climbed the stairs to the house. When she found the door open and the house empty, Linda was puzzled.

Dumping her purse and briefcase on the floor next to the desk, Linda walked over to the window and looked out at the beach. It was deserted, and Linda let out a sigh of frustration. Where was Scott off to now? His car was in the carport below the house; he couldn't have gone too far. Then, her eyes settled on something out in the water, bouncing and bobbing vigorously towards the shore. Within seconds, he was in full view.

Scott's blond hair was flying in the wind as the surfboard he was riding skimmed effortlessly across the water. His muscular young body leaned first one way and then the other, balancing his board against the force of the waves that carried him along.

Linda continued to watch him, entranced by the sight.

When Scott reached the shore, he jumped from the board and caught it in his hands. He looked up towards the house and waved a greeting.

A few minutes later, he bounded up the stairs and through the door, still dripping wet. "Hi, honey," he called out, shaking his hair. "You're early, aren't you?"

"Early?" Linda was stunned. "I almost got myself killed driving on your stupid freeways, and it took me almost two hours to get here."

"Hey, wait a minute," Scott protested. "They are not my freeways, and driving back and forth on them was your idea. I offered you a place to rest your weary head, but you refused."

Linda turned her back on him. She had made up her mind that she was not going to argue with Scott. For the sake of her script, she would get along with him if it killed her.

"You're right," Linda said as she turned around again. "It was my choice." She found she was talking to an empty room.

"Are you talking to me?" Scott yelled from the back of the house.

"Never mind," Linda shouted back.

"Help yourself to a cold drink," Scott said, his head appearing from around the wall that separated the kitchen from the short hallway.

Linda nodded and went into the kitchen, then helped herself to a glass of lemonade.

When Scott returned, dressed in a pair of shorts and a T-shirt, he found Linda sitting patiently on a sofa, sipping her drink. Her feet rested comfortably on the stack of magazines she had thrown to the floor.

Scott's hair was slicked back away from his face, which, Linda noted, he had shaved. His eyes sparkled like the ocean from which he had just emerged.

"So, are you ready to go to work?" he asked, flopping down beside her on the sofa.

"Yes, are you?"

"Believe it or not, I already have."

"You started without me?" Her tone was incredulous. How dare he start working on her screenplay without her!

"Don't worry. I didn't do much. Just made some notes on the background shots for the titles."

"What?" Linda wasn't sure what he was talking about.

"When you write a play," Scott explained, "the stage is set when the curtain rises. With a screenplay, you tell the camera what action to photograph to set the stage for the audience." Linda nodded, so he continued. "In this play, you started with the three guys meeting at Wally's Restaurant after work. That was fine, because you were restricted to a certain amount of space on the stage, but on the screen you can display all kinds of background information while the titles are rolling. Let me get my notes."

Scott jumped up, went over to the desk, and rummaged around a bit until he came up with a yellow legal pad.

"I don't know how you find anything in all that mess," Linda commented, taking another sip of her lemonade.

"Neither do I," Scott agreed. He handed Linda the notepad and then sat on the arm of the sofa and read it with her, explaining his notations. "See, I thought maybe we could start with some background color. Each guy leaving work, giving the audience an idea of their respective jobs. Wally getting ready for the dinner rush. The waitress calling in and quitting, leaving him in the lurch."

Linda quickly picked up his thoughts. "Then, go to Luanne getting ready to apply for the job at Wally's, all nervous and worried about going for it." Linda smiled, realizing that being released from the confines of the stage meant that her story could be expanded into something bolder and more thrilling.

"Yes," Scott agreed. "That's good. We show Luanne saying good-bye to Bobby, giving the audience a clue to his disability."

Several hours flew by as Linda and Scott worked on the script. They took turns pacing and typing, describing their ideas to one another.

"Sammy is so important," Linda told Scott after they drafted the first scene. "The actor has to be attractive, but not so much so that he makes the audience wonder why he's unsure of himself."

"Come on, Linda," Scott said, placing a friendly hand on her shoulder. "Don't get hung up on casting this early. That's someone else's job."

"But he's got to cast the right people for the parts," Linda continued insistently.

"And he will. Don't worry. Now that's enough work for our first day. How about a swim and some supper, in that order."

"Supper?" Linda glanced at her watch. It was after four. They had worked right through lunch and she hadn't even noticed. "I can't believe it's that late."

"This technical stuff takes a lot longer than you thought, doesn't it?" Scott teased.

Linda nodded and gave Scott a genuinely happy smile. They had a long way to go on this project, but they had worked well together today. That made all the difference for Linda. She was quickly gaining respect for Scott. It seemed he did know how to put a screenplay together.

"Scott, thank you," Linda said unexpectedly, surprising herself and Scott.

"For what?"

"For being nice to work with."

"Don't be so quick to pass out the compliments," Scott warned. "After the second day, I get lazy, and by next week, you'll need a ball and chain to keep me at the desk."

"Why? You're good and that makes it easy."

"Nope. You're the one with the talent. It's your script. I'm just helping with the technical end of it."

His eyes had suddenly lost their teasing sparkle, and he was looking at her so intently, so seriously, that it unnerved her more than ever.

Linda quickly looked away. "Do you have one of your scripts?" she asked. "I'd like to read something you've written and make my own judgement."

"No, ma'am," Scott replied. "I'd be embarrassed."

"Why?"

"Let's go for that swim. There are extra suits in the dresser in the guest room."

"That's okay," Linda said quickly. "I don't swim very well, and I think I'd better be getting back to town."

"Oh, no," Scott said firmly. "You made me work all day, and now I want to play. If you don't go back and change into a swimsuit, I'll throw you in the ocean with all your clothes on."

"You wouldn't."

"You know I would." Scott laughed, daring her to defy him.

"All right," Linda agreed. "I'm not looking forward to getting back on that miserable freeway anyway. I don't understand why it didn't seem that bad yesterday."

"Simple. You were with me, and nothing is too bad when I'm around." He winked at her. "Besides, we didn't drive during rush hour. If you hang around until after seven, you'll have no trouble driving back."

"And what about mornings? Do I have to leave at the break of dawn to avoid the traffic?"

"Probably, but if you don't want to do that, you can just move in here. The offer stands."

"I think I'll change now," Linda said, deliberately ignoring his last remark.

Scott followed her back to the guest room and pulled open the bottom drawer of the dresser. It held an assortment of bathing suits.

"There you go," he said. "I'll meet you on the beach."

Scott left, closing the door behind him, and Linda began sorting through the suits, trying to find one her size.

Where did he get all these? she wondered, as she discarded a skimpy bikini in favor of a more modest one-piece that looked like it might fit her.

Linda slipped into the suit and found that it fit pretty well. It was a bright shade of orange, and as she made her way down to the edge of the water, she felt a little like a neon sign flashing on the sand.

There were only a few scattered people along the beach. Scott had said that except for himself and the Cavanaughs, most of the houses were only used on weekends.

Scott let out a low appreciative whistle as she approached him. "You look great."

"Where did you get all those bathing suits?" Linda asked, feeling self-conscious under his admiring gaze.

"Carla used to own a boutique, and most of those are suits no one wanted to buy. We keep them here for visitors."

"I can understand why no one bought this one." Linda grimaced again at the flashy color.

Scott grabbed her hand, pulling her towards the water. Linda stiffened as the cold waves splashed across her bare feet and ankles.

"Come on," Scott urged. "Once you get all the way in, it's warm and wonderful."

"I told you before. I don't swim very well."

"Well, I do, and I promise not to let you drown. Anyway, this is salt water. All you have to do is relax and the water will keep you afloat."

Linda let herself be led out past the shoreline, and the coolness of the water washed over her. She had to admit it was refreshing. Scott kept a tight hold on her hand, and

Linda began to relax and enjoy the sensation of the waves pushing past her to reach the shore.

"Okay, lady," Scott said impishly when the water got past Linda's slim waistline and covered her chest. "Time for your swimming lesson."

Scott let go of her hand and dove under the water. He caught her around the waist. Linda screamed at his touch, and Scott came up roaring with laughter.

"What are you doing?" she yelled as he scooped her off her feet and laid her horizontally across the water, cradling her head and knees in his arms.

"I'm showing you how to float," Scott replied, but Linda was too frightened to relax. She threw her arms around his neck and hung on for dear life. "On second thought," Scott said, smiling down at her. "Did I mention that there were sharks out here?"

Linda's eyes filled with panic, and she opened and closed her mouth, but nothing came out. Her writer's imagination sent a vivid picture from the movie, *Jaws,* flashing across her mind. Instinctively, she drew her arms tighter around Scott's neck and pulled herself closer to him.

"Take me back to shore," she finally gasped, and the fear in her voice erased the smile from Scott's face.

"Hey, honey, I was just kidding. I'm sorry. I didn't mean to scare you."

Linda loosened her grip on his neck while at the same time Scott tightened his arms protectively, around her. He began to carry her back to shore. Linda's heart was beating rather fast, and she wasn't sure if it was her fear of the water, or the closeness of Scott.

"You can put me down," Linda ordered when they were about halfway in.

"Not until you're safely on land," Scott replied.

When he got to the edge of the water, Scott stopped walking and looked down at her face. Little droplets of water glistened on her cheeks. He brushed his lips softly across them.

Linda pulled away from him. "I can walk from here," she said firmly.

"I don't want to let go of you," Scott said. "But if you insist." He released her, letting her down slowly, until her feet rested on the sandy shore.

Linda's eyes were fixed on his face, waiting for him to speak. She felt the incoming waves pushing against her feet. Her ankles seemed anchored to the spot where Scott had placed her. There was a battle raging inside of her. Part of her wanted to feel the strength and safety of Scott's arms again, while another part was constructing a brick wall around her heart to keep him away.

Scott broke into a grin. "Don't look so frightened, Linda. The sharks won't come this close to the shore."

"What about the two-legged species?" Linda retorted, but instead of the casualness that she meant to imply, there was a huskiness that betrayed her vulnerability.

Linda forced her eyes away from his hypnotic stare and turned and ran away from him. Rush hour or not, she was going to leave the beach immediately.

"Now wait a minute," Scott called after her. "You're not really angry, are you?"

By the time Linda emerged from the bedroom, dressed in her jeans and blouse, she was in control again. She had rehearsed a neat little speech to put Scott in his place and make it clear that she was not there to play, but to work on her script. She found him in the kitchen, whistling and working on their supper.

"I'm not staying to eat," Linda announced, but Scott slipped the plate he was holding into the microwave.

"It's too late to back out now," he declared. "And you're going to love Carla's chicken Kiev. It's superb."

Linda continued into the living room to get her purse. Scott was right behind her, so she decided that this was the time to give him her speech.

"I want to get a few things straight," she began.

Scott held up his hand, and gave his own version. "This

is strictly a working relationship," he said. "And when the script is finished, the relationship will end. You want me to understand that I am not the kind of person you could become emotionally involved with, and therefore I am never to touch you again." He paused and grinned his infuriating grin. "Is that all?"

"That about sums it up," Linda said, ignoring the weak feeling she had in her knees as he walked closer to her.

"I'm sorry, honey. I know I come on too strong sometimes."

"And stop calling me 'Honey.' My name is Linda." Her voice held the same huskiness it had contained earlier, and Linda felt her control slipping away again. In a last effort to make her point, she jammed her purse under her arm, picked up her briefcase, and tried to push past Scott to the door.

He danced in front of her like a prize fighter, making it impossible for her to pass. "Linda, please. I'll behave. I promise. I'll keep my distance and respect your personal space. From now on, it's strictly business, but you can't walk out now. Think of that poor defenseless chicken spinning its heart out in the microwave. Doesn't he deserve the chance to grace your plate?"

Linda tried not smile, but she didn't succeed. "You really are quite nuts," she declared.

"And nuts like me don't grow on trees, you know."

The microwave beeped, and the smell of the food did the rest. Linda tossed her things on a nearby chair.

"Where's the paper plates?" she asked.

"Coming right up," Scott promised.

Their conversation over dinner, which, as Scott promised, was superb, led to a renewed effort on the script, and it was well past nine o'clock when they stopped working and Scott walked Linda out to her car.

"Are you sure you can find your way back in the dark?" Scott asked. "You could . . ."

"Don't you dare ask me to stay here again," Linda ordered.

"Yes, ma'am. I'd rather cut out my tongue and have it for lunch."

"You're very dramatic," Linda said. "You should have been an actor."

"I am an actor," Scott replied softly. "Right this minute, I'm acting like being near you doesn't affect me at all, when in reality, it's driving me crazy."

"I'd better leave." Linda opened the car door and slipped quickly inside.

Scott leaned through the open window. "I scared you again, didn't I? Well, it's okay. I'm a little scared myself."

"You're just too unconventional for me," Linda admitted. "But you are a darn good writer, and I do like working with you."

"Wow, I've never been admired for my mind before."

"I'll see you tomorrow." Linda started the engine.

"I'll look forward to it." Scott backed away from the car.

The freeways were flowing nicely at this hour, and Linda arrived at her hotel in less than an hour. She was exhausted.

It had been a day full of surprises. She had not expected Scott to be such a talented writer, and she had been totally unprepared for the strong feelings being in his arms had aroused in her.

Forget it, Linda, she told herself sternly. He may be charming and talented and gorgeous, but he's still a bum. If he had any ambition he wouldn't isolate himself at that beach house without a telephone or any other contact with the outside world. You love the bright lights and excitement of the city. There's no way you could have a relationship with a man like him.

Chapter Seven

The rest of the week passed quickly. Linda and Scott continued to work well together, but the movie script was moving along rather slowly. By Friday afternoon, Scott and Linda decided to let it rest until Monday and to take the weekend off.

"I've never had this problem before," Linda complained as she prepared to leave the beach house. "I usually have so many ideas, I can't get them down on paper fast enough."

"It's my fault," Scott told her. "It always happens to me. I guess that's why I have so many unfinished projects."

The serious tone of his voice made Linda want to cheer him up. "Scott, you've been terrific. It's just my inexperience that's holding us down. You know what? I think you're deliberately holding back some of your ideas because you don't want me to feel threatened."

Scott rewarded her comment with one of his dazzling smiles. "I wish that were true, my dear, but unfortunately, it's not. We've written ourselves into a corner on that last scene, and I can't think of a clever way to get us out of it."

"I never thought that Dancer's requests for a few changes would be so hard to do."

"It will work," Scott assured her. "Your story is great, and we'll find a way to make everything fit together."

"Maybe I'm just having a hard time twisting my original character into another dimension."

"I don't think that's the problem, it's . . ." The sound of a car door slamming interrupted Scott's thought. "We've got company." He opened the door and looked out. "It's Carla. You haven't met her yet, have you?"

"No," Linda answered. "I haven't." She backed away from the door, waiting for Scott's sister to make her entrance.

Carla made her way up the stairs, carrying a tuxedo on a hanger in one hand and balancing a large box between her other arm and one slim hip. She was blond, the same height as Scott, and strikingly beautiful. Apparently, good looks ran in the family.

"Hi, little brother." Carla's voice was as silky smooth as expensive velvet. "I brought a fresh food supply, and your suit for the party."

"What party?" Scott asked, taking the box from her and carrying it into the kitchen.

Carla called after him. "The premiere, darling. It's tomorrow night. Don't tell me you forgot. Yes, of course you did, and we couldn't call and remind you because you don't believe in modern conveniences like telephones." Carla suddenly noticed Linda standing there. "You must be Linda. I'm Carla Dancer, Scott's sister. I've been looking forward to meeting you."

"And I you," Linda said, taking the lovely, perfectly manicured hand Carla offered her.

Scott returned from the kitchen, took the tuxedo that Carla was dangling impatiently in front of him, and laid it on the sofa.

"And you are to wear that, Scott," Carla warned. "Don't you dare show up in one of your weird outfits. Frank will have a breakdown."

"You know I hate going to these things, so why don't

you just take your tuxedo back to wherever you rented it," Scott replied.

"I didn't rent it, darling. I bought it for you. It's time you took your proper place on the Hollywood scene. I'm tired of everyone asking where you are all the time."

"Frank left a message at my hotel saying he's sending a car to pick me up," Linda interjected. "Perhaps you could tell him how much I appreciate his thinking of me."

"Dancer Productions wants you to enjoy your stay here," Carla said with a smile that was as disarming as Scott's.

"Tell Frank he doesn't need me there," Scott proclaimed.

Carla turned and gave him a menacing look. It was obvious that the two siblings were about to have an argument, and Linda didn't want to be a witness to it. "Well, I have to be going," she said quickly, moving towards the door. "I still haven't figured out what I'm going to wear tomorrow night. It's been lovely meeting you, Carla."

"With your coloring, you'd look smashing in white," Carla said. "Go to Pierre's on Rodeo Drive and pick out a dress. I'll call and tell them to charge it to my husband. That's the least Frank can do for you, since he's expecting you to be Scott's date, and it looks like you'll have to drag him there kicking and screaming."

This news came as a complete surprise to Linda, but before she could comment, Scott did. "Oh, I get it. Frank's using the premiere as an opportunity to publicize Linda's movie." He turned and looked at Linda. "In that case, I'll wear the monkey suit and pick you up in Frank's car. His driver is used to my kicking and screaming."

"Excellent," Carla said. "Then it's all settled."

"I guess so," Linda murmured, looking back at Scott. He was standing there in his cutoff shorts and bare feet, wearing a T-shirt that advertised a name-brand beer. Seeing him in a tuxedo would be quite a change.

"Now, Linda," Carla continued. "When I get home, I'll call Pierre's and arrange everything. All you'll have to do is show up and pick out a dress. Maybe you'd better do it first thing in the morning. You're so petite, they may need a little extra time to do alterations."

Linda nodded obediently.

Scott flopped down on the sofa next to the tuxedo. "My sister loves to arrange things." Scott's remark was softened by the affection in his voice.

"Someone in the family has to be organized," Carla retorted. "I'd better check on the frozen food I carried in. Scott probably put it in the oven." She hurried off to the kitchen.

"Good-bye," Linda called after her. "I'll see you tomorrow night."

The next morning, Linda felt like a princess as Pierre himself helped her select a dress for the premiere. As Carla suggested, Linda settled on a white gown. It had a halter style neckline that was properly modest yet accentuated Linda's figure. The back of the dress dipped dangerously low, exposing the creamy smoothness of her back, and then draped nicely over her hips. It flared out just enough to be comfortable for walking, sitting, or dancing.

The dress needed to be shortened, but Pierre promised that it would be done and delivered to her hotel in plenty of time for the premiere.

Linda's next stop was the beauty salon, where her coal-black hair was done in a cute but stylish flip, and her nails were buffed and polished with a subtle shade of peach.

On the way back to the hotel, Linda stopped at a small jewelry store and splurged on a necklace that looked like strands of spun silver, with sparkling earrings to match.

At 7:00, the hotel clerk called to say that Scott was on his way up to her room. Linda was just putting the finishing touches on her makeup. She was pleased with her appearance. For the first time in her life, the girl who had grown up in a poor neighborhood in Brooklyn felt as elegant and rich as she looked.

There was a loud rap on the door, and Linda ran to answer it. The sight of Scott standing there in his tuxedo made her mouth fall open in surprise.

"You look gorgeous," Linda cried, unable to suppress her feelings.

"I feel like a sardine stuffed into this suit, but it's worth it just to get a look at you in that dress," Scott said with a stare.

"Thank you, sir," Linda replied gaily. "And thank you for being my escort. I have to admit, I'm a little nervous."

A few minutes later, they emerged from the hotel. "That's our car?" Linda exclaimed as the driver opened the door of a sleek black limousine parked at the curb.

"Afraid so," Scott quipped. "They were all out of Volkswagen Beetles."

The driver helped Linda into the backseat of the car. "My first *apartment* wasn't this big," she whispered to Scott.

He laughed. "It's all part of the charade."

Linda looked at him curiously, wondering why he felt so strongly about his own lifestyle. She had never met anyone who was so unconcerned with money or what it could buy. Maybe because he'd never really faced an empty refrigerator or had to worry about paying the rent.

They arrived at the theater and the chauffeur dutifully helped Linda alight from the car. Scott stood at attention, waiting for her. Cameras flashed around them, and Linda clung to Scott's arm, blinded by the lights but very happy to be there. *This is what I've worked for,* she thought. *This is what I've always wanted.*

Linda had attended many theater premieres in New York, but never as an honored guest, like tonight, and never had she experienced the glitter and fever-pitched excitement for which Hollywood was famous.

Floodlights crossed the sky over the theater, and music from the movie they were about to see was playing over a loud-speaker. Reporters wanted to interview them, but a uniformed guard ushered them into the lobby where Frank and Carla were waiting for them.

"You both look fabulous," Carla cried as they approached. She looked rather fabulous too—she wore a black gown covered with silver sequins that sparkled like diamonds with her every move.

Carla hugged both Linda and Scott, and Frank greeted Linda as if she were his long-lost sister. Linda felt very important as they were led to a podium. Frank stepped up to the microphone to say a few words for the press people who had been allowed inside the theater.

Frank Dancer was a bit overweight and his hairline was receding, but he still looked impressive in a tuxedo with red satin lapels that matched his bow tie and contrasted with his pale pink ruffled shirt.

In a booming voice, Frank thanked everyone for being there, then introduced some of the celebrities in attendance, including, of course, the stars of the movie.

Linda was so mesmerized by the entire scene that she didn't realize that Dancer was talking about her and Scott when he began telling the crowd about the marvelous new writing team that was penning his next film.

"And here they are, taking a little time off from their work to be with us tonight, the lovely Linda Lucas and her co-writer, Scott Richards."

Linda heard the applause and Scott nudged her. They stepped out from where they had been standing to take a bow. The whole experience was having a dizzying effect on Linda, and she didn't mind Scott's strong arm slipping around her waist. She needed the support.

After the big buildup, Frank's new movie was not as good as Linda expected, and she found herself worrying about how successful her film was going to be.

The theater was dark. Scott was slumped into the seat next to her, obviously bored with the movie. On an impulse, Linda reached out and touched his arm. Scott sat up, took hold of her hand, and kept it captive for the rest of the movie.

The warmth of his fingers encircling her own made Linda remember how safe she had felt in his arms when he was carrying her back to shore, and a spark of longing returned to claim her thoughts.

Since that first day, Scott had kept his promise and been a perfect gentleman, but Linda was no longer sure that she wanted him to remain that way. Spending so much time with him at the beach was beginning to wear down her resistance to his good looks and offbeat charm.

Linda couldn't deny her attraction to Scott was growing stronger, but it was more than just physical. There was also a mutual respect and admiration growing between them. Their working relationship was good, and it was spilling over to enhance their personal feelings as well.

"I'm glad that's over with," Scott told Linda when they were back in the limousine on their way to the party. "If Frank keeps turning out bombs like that one, Carla will have to hock her mink coat."

"I didn't think it was that bad," Linda said defensively.

"Yes, you did," Scott insisted. "Say, how about skipping the party and going out for pizza? I'm starving."

"Absolutely not." Linda was appalled that he could even suggest such a thing. "I've been looking forward to this party all week."

"You really like this phony glitter, don't you?"

"I love it, and frankly I don't understand why you don't. You act as if fame and fortune were a disease that you're afraid of being infected with."

Scott laughed at her assessment of him. "I'm sorry my lack of ambition bugs you so much, but I think you have enough for both of us."

"And what is that supposed to mean?" she asked, becoming annoyed with his attitude.

"Well, maybe it means that I'm beginning to think of us as a couple."

Linda had just started to reply when the car came to a halt in front of Frank and Carla's home in Beverly Hills. She stared out the window at the house, once again in awe of what she was seeing.

The house was three stories high and big enough to be a hotel. Once inside, Linda insisted that Scott take her on a brief tour of the downstairs. He obliged, and together they walked from room to enormous room. There was a library and a game room, and separate offices and sitting rooms for both Frank and Carla. The catering staff had barricaded the kitchen doors, but Scott assured her that it was as large and well-equipped as the White House kitchen.

Finally, they arrived back at the foyer which led into the dining room and the adjacent ballroom that opened onto a terrace that then led to the swimming pool and gardens. Linda was as wide-eyed as a child on Christmas morning.

"Where have you two been?" Frank asked when Scott and Linda walked through the door of the ballroom. The orchestra was playing, and people were already dancing or in the dining room filling their plates from long tables laden with food.

"Scott was showing me the house," Linda said breathlessly. "It's incredible."

"It used to belong to Hedda Hopper; she was famous for her big celebrity parties," Frank replied, and began naming some of the old movie stars who had once frequented the house.

While Frank and Linda chatted, a girl with platinum blond hair that hung perfectly straight from the top of her head all the way down to her waist appeared and pulled Scott out on the dance floor.

"All the girls love Scott," Dancer commented, and then said, as if he were issuing her a warning, "but Scott's not the type to settle down and support a family."

Linda nodded, but was spared from making a comment by the arrival of Charlie and LaVerne. Frank greeted them and then excused himself to greet some other new arrivals. The elderly couple turned their attention to Linda.

"Hey, chickadee," Charlie said, grabbing Linda's hand and shaking it vigorously.

"He forgot your name," LaVerne said.

"Hi, Charlie," Linda said. "I'm Linda."

"Of course you are. I remembered. It's LaVerne who has memory lapses."

"I'm not the one who forgot where he parked the car,"

LaVerne replied. "That's why we're late. How are you, Linda?"

"I'm fine. It's nice to see you again."

"I thought Scott would bring you down for dinner some night."

"Why would he want to do that?" Charlie asked her. "One of your home-cooked meals would have her on the next plane back to New York City."

LaVerne laughed. "He's right, but I know a good caterer. Where's Scott? We'll set a date right now."

"He's dancing," Linda said, pointing to Scott and the blond.

The musicians had moved into a lively rock tune, and Scott and his partner attracted some attention as they cavorted around the floor doing some of the latest steps.

"Looks more like they got ants in their britches," Charlie said. "Come on, ladies. Let's find the food."

"You two go on," Linda said. "I'll wait for Scott."

"He's worth waiting for," LaVerne told her softly. "Scott is a little crazy, but he's a real sweetheart."

"Here's an idea," Charlie said. "You girls keep yakking and I'll eat next Tuesday."

"Oh, come on, you old coot," LaVerne said. "I'll see you later, Linda."

"Not if she sees you first," Charlie told her.

"I hope that buffet table has plenty of ice. You need some cooling off, hotshot." LaVerne retorted.

Linda put a hand over her mouth to keep from laughing out loud. Charlie and LaVerne seemed to thrive on insulting each other, but it was done with so much underlying affection, no one could feel uncomfortable or take offense at their outrageous remarks.

Scott was still dancing, so Linda walked around the perimeter of the dance floor and went out to the patio where a white-clad waiter handed her a glass of champagne.

The patio was lit with soft twinkling lights, and the air was filled with the scent of flowers blooming in the gardens that surrounded it.

There were a number of people milling around the pool, drinking and eating. Linda felt content to just stand in the shadows and watch them.

Then, Scott came up next to her, took the champagne glass out of her hand, and tossed it into the shrubs. Without a word, he guided her back to the dance floor. The orchestra was playing a slow, dreamy song.

"Why didn't you come out and rescue me?" he whispered in her ear as they swayed to the music. "Didn't you get the signals I was sending you?"

"Signals? I thought they were part of your dance routine," Linda said. "You certainly seemed to be enjoying yourself."

"I always look like I'm enjoying myself at a party, but I'm not."

"Oh, Scott, you say the dumbest things." Linda stiffened as his hand moved intimately down the curve of her bare back.

"You're right. Like the other night when I promised not to touch you again."

"We held hands in the theater," Linda countered. "And you're touching me now."

"I know, but not the way I want to touch you," he whispered back. Using his forefinger, he lifted her chin so he could look into her eyes. Linda's breath caught in her chest. He looked so handsome tonight, it was an effort not to melt into his strong arms. "Are you going to hold me to that promise?" he asked.

"I don't know," she answered honestly, lowering her gaze. Looking into his eyes was too dangerous tonight.

Scott chuckled softly and pulled her closer. She could feel his heart beating next to her burning skin. "Does that mean you're weakening?" he persisted.

Before Linda could answer, Frank and Carla danced by and engaged them in some small talk. Linda was grateful that she didn't have to answer Scott's last question, but she knew he would be asking it again.

The rest of the evening passed too quickly for Linda. As

the crowd began to loosen up, the party went into full swing. An assortment of women, young, old, and in-between kept taking Scott off to dance with them. He appeared to revel in the attention they lavished on him.

Frank and Carla took Linda around and introduced her to several interesting people, including some other screenwriters. While Scott was occupied with his admirers, Linda was having a very enjoyable evening and spent a considerable amount of time on the dance floor herself.

When the orchestra leader announced the last dance of the evening, Linda was whirled onto the floor by a charming young actor who Carla had introduced her to just moments before.

His name was Kevin, and he was an excellent dancer, but Linda was wondering where Scott was. She hadn't seen him for the past half hour or so.

"Excuse me, old man." Linda heard Scott's voice next to her ear. "We're cutting in."

Scott had the long-haired blond in tow, and Kevin didn't seem to mind changing partners. But before he danced off with the blond, he asked Linda if he could call her sometime.

"I'd like that," Linda said sweetly.

Scott practically lifted Linda off her feet as he whisked her away from Kevin. "A two-legged shark if I ever saw one," Scott said sternly.

"Oh, really," Linda replied. "I thought he was rather attractive. And speaking of sharks, you've had a number of them swimming around you tonight."

"Not anymore. They're all mad at me."

"Really. Why?"

"I told them that you and I were living together."

"You what?" Linda asked the question so loudly that several people glanced in their direction, and this amused Scott immensely. "How dare you say that," Linda said in a calmer tone.

"I'm not just saying that. It's the truth, or at least it will be. I'm taking you home with me tonight."

"I don't think so," Linda fumed, trying to pull herself free from his arms, but Scott only tightened his hold on her.

"Now, Linda, wait a minute. You're not giving me a chance to explain. Right away, you're thinking that I'm taking you home to seduce you, and though the thought is always on my mind, that is not the reason."

"Then, what is the reason?" Linda was considering a well-placed kick in the shins to make him let go of her.

"It's because Frank just told me that we have to have the script finished in two weeks."

"Two weeks? That's impossible. I don't believe he said that."

"Go ask him yourself."

Linda looked around the dance floor trying to spot Frank, but he was nowhere in sight. She looked up at Scott. "Why would he say that?"

"The director he wants for the film stopped in for a drink and told Frank he needs to confirm his schedule and has a number of other projects he's considering. He never commits to a project until he's read the finished script, so either he gets it in the next two weeks and puts it on his schedule, or he fills his schedule with something else."

The music ended and everyone applauded the orchestra except for Linda. She stood stock-still, staring at Scott. "How can we complete the script in two weeks?" she cried. "We've been stuck on one scene for two days."

"That's why I want you to move out to the beach house. We'll have to work around the clock to get the script ready in time."

"Why can't Frank just get another director?"

"He can, but believe me, Linda, you don't want another director. This guy is great, and he'll be so good with this script. Please, trust me on this. I know how much this film means to you, and it's begun to mean a lot to me too."

Linda shook her head and pulled away from Scott. She hurried off the dance floor and took refuge on the patio. What Scott said made sense, but there was no way she could stay at the beach house with him. Falling in love with Scott Richards was not an option. He was too crazy, too unpredictable, and Linda already felt her emotions slipping out of control. She had to keep her distance. She also had to finish her screenplay.

"What's wrong, honey?" a voice said from the shadows. "Did Scott do something to upset you?" Linda spun around and faced LaVerne, who was moving closer with a look of genuine concern on her face. "Do I have to send Charlie over to straighten him out?"

"No. It's not Scott. It's me."

"Thank goodness. Charlie couldn't straighten out a paper clip."

Linda laughed and then felt tears spring to her eyes.

"Hey. Something *is* wrong. Come on, I've got shoes older than you. Maybe I can help."

Linda quickly explained the situation to LaVerne. "I know you're very fond of Scott, but he and I are like oil and water, and I don't think moving into his beach house would work for either of us."

"Oh, heck. I thought you were going to give me a real problem to solve. This one is a piece of cake. Charlie and I have tons of space. You can stay with us while you finish the script. I'll be your chaperone. I raised two boys, always wanted a girl to look out for."

Two hours later, Scott and Linda carried her luggage into Charlie and LaVerne's guest room. It was a delightful room with its own bath. A big feather bed piled high with pillows and a downy soft comforter stood against one wall. Mismatched tables and chairs that were probably antiques were arranged to form a sitting room of sorts. The overall effect was one of warmth and comfort.

Charlie and LaVerne were in the kitchen arguing over whether to serve hot chocolate or coffee to their new houseguest.

Scott and Linda went out to the patio to wait for the refreshments. It was cool by the ocean, and Linda shivered as sprays of salt water hung in the air.

"It'll be hot chocolate," Scott told her. "LaVerne serves hot chocolate for every occasion."

"It's so nice of them to let me stay here," Linda said. "I offered to pay rent, but Charlie had a fit."

"I'm sure he did." Scott smiled at her. "When the hot chocolate arrives, we'll all drink to the success of the script and they'll be happy as clams to be a part of the process."

Linda nodded.

"Get that worried look off your face," Scott said cheerfully. "Everything is going to work out. We'll get the script finished in time."

Linda gave him a weak smile and walked over to look out at the ocean. It was dark and she couldn't see the beach, but she could hear the waves crashing against the shore.

It wasn't the script Linda was worried about. She had worked under short deadlines before. It was the fact that staying at the beach, even in another house, meant that she would be totally on Scott's territory for the next few weeks, and that had her terrified.

As much as Linda was trying to fight against it, she knew that she was falling under his spell. Scott's magnetism was as strong as the tide that sent the ocean rushing over the sand, and in a very short time Linda might find herself in over her head.

Chapter Eight

Linda awoke to the smell of coffee brewing. There was no clock in the room, so she felt around on the table next to her until her fingers closed over her watch. She positioned it over her face and read the time.

"Ten o'clock," she said out loud. "That can't be right."

Linda sat up, pushed herself free of the softness of the bedcovers, and moved to the windows that faced the ocean. The sun was already high in the sky. "It's so beautiful and peaceful here," she whispered. "I can understand why Scott loves it."

There was a knock on her door. "Hey, sleepyhead," Scott called out. "Are you in there?"

"Yes," Linda called back.

"Well, get a move on. You're setting a bad example for me."

"I'll be there in a minute," Linda promised.

"Take ten. LaVerne said she'd feed me."

Linda dashed for the bathroom. She was dressed and ready to go in the allotted ten minutes. "Tomorrow I set an alarm clock," she promised herself.

She turned and looked in the ornate gold-rimmed mirror attached to the back of the closet door and made a face at herself. She hadn't had time to shampoo out yesterday's fancy hairdo, and it looked strange with the T-shirt and

53

shorts she was wearing. "Do I brush it out, or leave it?" she asked herself. Then, shaking her head and turning away from her reflection, she scolded herself, "Stop talking to yourself and go out and face him."

Linda quickly made the bed and emerged from the room. The hallway and living room were empty, but she could hear laughter coming from the kitchen.

Scott was at the table with LaVerne. He was clad in swimming trunks, with a towel draped casually across his shoulders. Apparently, he had been surfing or swimming before coming to the house to get her. His hair was still wet, slicked back from his handsome face. He looked bronze and healthy, like he had just stepped out of the pages of a fitness magazine. Linda had to force her eyes away from him.

LaVerne was dressed in a long flowing housedress with pastel stripes. She had tissue paper wrapped around her head in an effort to preserve her hairdo from the night before. She was in the middle of a story.

"Bob took me out after the show that night. We went to this nightclub near the theater. Delores came out, sang one song, and Bob was a goner. Dropped me faster than you can snap your fingers. That's how I got stuck with Charlie."

Scott looked up at Linda. "LaVerne used to date Bob Hope."

"Really?"

"Really," LaVerne said without a smile. "He sends me a fruitcake every Christmas."

"You are a fruitcake." Charlie's muffled yell came from another room. "Come open this dang door."

"Have some breakfast, Linda," LaVerne said, pushing herself away from the table. "Charlie's locked himself in the closet again."

Scott and Linda exchanged a smile as LaVerne hurried out of the kitchen.

"What's Charlie doing in the closet?" Linda asked.

"Looking for some hat Bob Hope gave him at a golf tournament. It's actually a storage room and it's got enough stuff crammed in it from their show business days to fill a museum."

"Wow. I'd like to see some of it."

"Don't worry, you will, but not today. Get your breakfast to go. I woke up with a great idea for the script. We need to work it out and get it down on paper before I lose it."

Linda nodded, quickly poured herself a mug of coffee, and grabbed a doughnut from the box on the table. She and Scott yelled their good-byes to LaVerne and Charlie.

"Don't forget about going out to dinner tonight. We're trying a new Chinese place," LaVerne called back.

"Sure," Scott said. "We'll be back at seven."

"Okay. Dress casual."

Scott and Linda strolled down the beach. Linda moved slowly, trying to sip her coffee and eat her doughnut while treading on the sandy path. She should have been thinking about the script and the day's work ahead of them. Instead she was thinking about how natural it seemed to be making plans for dinner with Scott and the Cavanaughs.

"How come you agreed to go out to dinner?" Linda asked suddenly. "I thought you didn't like to leave the beach."

"I don't. I'm trying to make you happy."

"Why?"

"Lots of reasons that we won't get into right now. Unless, of course, you want to skip work today and just sit on the beach with me."

"You know we can't do that," Linda replied.

"Right. So we'll just work and talk about my reasons some other time."

They had reached the beach house. Scott stopped and motioned for Linda to climb the stairs ahead of him. She ran up the stairs and pushed the door open. She went directly to the desk while Scott went into the kitchen to make a fresh pot of coffee.

The last script pages they had been working on were on the desk. Linda immediately sat down and read them over. The dialogue still sounded stiff and clichéd. Then, another problem presented itself. She had left the hotel without leaving a forwarding address or phone number where she could be reached. The Cavanaughs were doing enough for her. She didn't want to take advantage by making them field her phone calls too. Perhaps she could drive into town and buy a cell phone.

Then she remembered that she no longer had a rental car. She had turned the keys in to the hotel clerk when she checked out last night.

Thoroughly disgusted with herself, Linda got up and began to pace. Last night, she had been so flustered about spending more time at the beach with Scott that she hadn't given the other inconveniences of staying at the beach any consideration.

"Coffee will be ready in a few minutes," Scott said as he came into the room.

"I need to go into town," Linda told him.

"Why?"

"To get a cell phone."

"No way. Against house rules," Scott replied cheerfully. "Besides, it probably won't work out here." He walked past her and sat at the desk.

"I don't want to bother Charlie and LaVerne with my business calls. I will only turn it on when I call out to check my messages. I assume Frank will take calls at his office for me."

"Already arranged." Scott grinned at her. "Julie will call the Cavanaughs every evening and deliver your messages there."

"Julie? Frank's secretary?"

"One and the same."

"What if Charlie answers the phone? I don't think he's a reliable message taker."

"He's not incompetent, just a bit eccentric. He takes my messages."

"You get messages?"

Scott laughed. "Sometimes two or three a month. Everyone knows that they can reach me by leaving a message at

Frank's office. Julie relays them to Charlie's house, and Charlie delivers them to me."

Linda looked doubtful. "I have friends, I have an agent in New York . . . I have . . ."

"I know that. That's why I called Frank's office from Charlie's this morning and asked Julie to take your calls. She's going to call the hotel and your agent and make sure everyone knows how to reach you. You won't miss any calls. I promise."

"Well, I guess that will be okay. I just hate to impose on Julie and Charlie and LaVerne."

"Part of Julie's job is to help the writers and other people working with Frank. As for Charlie and LaVerne, they're on my payroll."

"Your payroll?" Linda asked, grinning at him.

"Pineapple upside down cake. They get one every month even if I don't get any messages. The bakery next to Frank's office makes them for me when Carla is too busy."

"Sounds like a fair wage," Linda said. "I guess you've got it all covered. Thank you."

"You're welcome. Now we'd better get to work. I thought you were never going to get your lazy bones out of bed today."

Linda stared at him as he picked up the script pages she had just read through. He scanned them briefly and then tore them in half and dropped them on top of an already overflowing wastebasket. The sun coming in from the windows behind him danced across his broad bronze shoulders and made the ocean spray that still clung to his blond curls glisten.

"Aren't you going to get dressed?" Linda asked. Her concern about the telephone was forgotten. The only thing she could think of was how wonderful he looked and how much she wanted to rush across the room and touch him.

"Oh, yeah," Scott said with a crooked smile. "Sorry. I keep forgetting how formal you New Yorkers are."

Linda darted out of his path as he made his way towards the back of the house. When he was out of the room, she counted slowly to ten and went over to the desk and turned on the computer. With a few deft keystrokes, she brought up the script pages Scott had just ripped in two and line by line eliminated them from the screen. Then she read over the last few pages of the preceding scene.

Scott returned, dressed in a pair of tight jeans that were almost as revealing as his bathing suit. Fortunately, he had also donned a loose-fitting shirt with a colorful array of parrots flying in all directions. Looking at it made Linda a little dizzy. She shook her head and turned back to the computer screen.

"I'm waiting to hear your idea," she told Scott. "I hope it was a way to rewrite the scene we just trashed."

"No. It's a scene between Tom and Kathy. I woke up thinking that those two characters are a lot like you and I."

"How is that?"

"Kathy is a go-getter. Tom is a bum."

"Tom is not a bum," Linda said. "He has a job."

"I wasn't talking about his profession. I was referring to his attitude about life. He's content to take life as it comes. He complains when it doesn't go his way, but he doesn't do much to try and change things. Kathy, on the other hand, tries to control everything."

"Are you accusing me of being a control freak?" Linda asked.

"Not exactly, but you have to admit you like to have things planned out in advance. You set goals and then map out the steps necessary to meet those goals."

"And what's wrong with that?"

"Nothing. Except." Scott shrugged and smiled at her.

"Except what?" Linda scowled back at him.

"Great." Scott's smile grew broader. "Now you're really annoyed with me. Keep that edge and let's work on the scene with Tom and Kathy at the bowling alley. You take Kathy's part and I'll be Tom."

Linda sat down at the computer and began typing in the scene as they reworked the original dialogue from the play. Her fingers flew across the keyboard as she and Scott became the characters in the script. Linda found she was able to transfer the level of irritation she was feeling for Scott to the page and as she did, Kathy's dialogue became sharper and more dynamic.

When they finished the three-page scene, Linda read it over again. The attraction the two characters felt for each other seemed enhanced by the new antagonism they had managed to work into the scene.

"It works," Linda said simply.

"An old trick I learned in a writing class. Of course you can't do it without a good partner to take the other side."

"You took writing classes?" Linda was surprised by his admission. "I thought you were too spontaneous to do anything that structured."

Scott laughed. "I took a few classes. I was too unstructured to take them seriously, but a few things rubbed off. Now what should we do about the other scene Frank asked us to change?"

"I think we should forget about it for now."

"I knew you'd think of something," he replied, smiling encouragement.

"We skip the scene we were having problems with and go on to the next one in the outline. As we forge ahead, we're bound to figure out how to go back and make it right."

"Now you're thinking like a director. Film scenes are rarely shot in the same sequence as the script."

"If that's a compliment, thank you."

"It wasn't. You look really sexy with that elegant hairdo from last night contrasting with the casual clothes you're wearing today. That's a compliment."

Linda laughed. "Let's get to work."

The afternoon flew by as they continued to work on the script, munching on chips and pretzels instead of stopping for a proper lunch.

By the time the sun was moving down towards the horizon, they had drafted three more scenes and Linda felt like her writing rhythm was working again. She was at the keyboard and Scott was lounging on the sofa, making paper airplanes and sailing them across the room whenever they came up with a piece of dialogue or descriptive phrase he liked.

Linda would have liked to keep working, but Scott reminded her of their dinner date with Charlie and LaVerne. "It will do us good to take a break. We can work on it when we get back, if you're not too tired."

"I'm impressed. I thought you were going to suggest a moonlight swim or a clam dig for our after-dinner activity."

Scott aimed his last paper airplane directly at Linda's lovely hairdo and hit his target. "See how you tend to misjudge people?"

Linda ignored his last remark and concentrated on saving the script pages they'd completed on the computer's hard drive, and again on a backup disk. Then she got up and began picking up the paper airplanes that had settled in various spots around the room. Stomping her foot into the wastebasket, she made room for the planes on top of the other trash.

When her task was completed, she turned back to Scott, who was still sprawled on the sofa. "What should I wear for dinner?"

"How about that backless number you had on last night," Scott replied. "I liked that a lot."

"Only if you're wearing your tux again," Linda countered.

"Ouch . . . What you've got on will be fine. Although I think Charlie said the head of Disney was going to be there."

"Disney Studios?"

"Or Disneyland." Scott shrugged. "One or the other."

"At the Chinese place?"

"Right."

"When did he tell you that?"

"This morning when I came over to wake you up. That's why he was looking for the hat from Bob Hope. He wants to wear it to the restaurant and impress the guy. They're casting a new movie and Charlie wants a part in it."

Linda glanced at her watch. It was 5:30. Scott pushed himself off the couch and put his arm around her shoulder. "Time for a swim. Are you coming?"

"No, thank you," Linda said brightly. "I have to figure out what to wear—either my blue dress or some jeans and my Mickey Mouse sweatshirt."

Scott liked her joke and rewarded her with one of his stunning smiles. Then, he began to peel off his own jeans to reveal that he still wore his swimsuit underneath them. Instead of unbuttoning his shirt, he pulled it over his head and tossed it and the jeans onto the sofa.

Linda resisted the urge to pick up after him. She waved good-bye as he bounded out the door and then walked over to the window to watch him run across the sand towards the water.

He's like a kid playing grown-up, she told herself, as Scott picked up speed and ran into the wave that was cresting towards the shore. "I wish I could be more like him," she admitted out loud.

Chapter Nine

The new Chinese place turned out to be a Japanese restaurant with private rooms. They passed through the main dining room that was authentically decorated with painted lacquer screens which afforded secluded alcoves. Lanterns etched with flowers, birds, and tree branches illuminated the room and gave it a warm cozy glow.

At the door to their private dining room, the hostess instructed them to remove their shoes. The table inside the room was sunken, with cushioned benches on all four sides.

Scott held Linda's hand as she stepped down. She seated herself on the bench and let her bare toes explore the cool smooth tiles beneath the table.

"You'll need a crane to get me out of here," Charlie complained as he sank down on the bench opposite Linda.

"Thanks for helping me," LaVerne said, standing on the edge and looking down at her husband. She swiped at the golf cap Charlie had planted on his head and knocked it off.

Scott hurried over and assisted LaVerne, then took his place next to Linda. LaVerne was still glaring at Charlie, who was trying to position the golf cap at the right angle again.

"Sorry, doll baby," Charlie said. "But you're so young and agile, I didn't think you needed help."

"You're excused," LaVerne said. "Now take that hat off. It's impolite to wear a hat inside a building."

Charlie nodded, obediently removed the hat from his head, and placed it on the table next to him. "If I have to, I'll give it to Mac to get that part."

"Mac is the man from Disney?" Linda asked.

"He doesn't work at Disney," LaVerne explained. "He's an independent producer who just sold a film to Disney Studios. Charlie thinks taking him to dinner and giving him a hat will get him a part in the movie. I say he'd have a better shot by waiting until we throw our luau party and asking him then."

"If he doesn't give me a part tonight, I'm not inviting him to the luau," Charlie said.

LaVerne sighed and shook her head. "This man is as stubborn as an old mule."

"Charlie," Scott said. "If you really want a part in a movie, I'll talk to Frank. He's casting several films in the next few months."

"Maybe you can get a part in our movie," Linda suggested.

"How about you, LaVerne?" Scott asked. "Are you interested in doing some film work?"

"No way," LaVerne said. "I've had my days in the limelight. Stage work, film work, I've done it all, now it's time for fun in the sun. If I had it to do over again, I'd work less and play more. Like you, Scott."

"Thanks, LaVerne. It's nice to know that one woman in my life shares my views." He looked at Linda.

Linda gave him a long steady gaze, and was about to make a comment, when the guest of honor arrived. Mac was short for MacKenzie Cohen. Linda had never heard of him, and by the time dinner was over, she realized why.

The man was quiet and withdrawn. Trying to make conversation with Mac was like trying to force an elephant through the eye of a needle.

They ordered an authentic Japanese dinner for five and it was superb. Beef and chicken simmered in a variety of spicy sauces were served with rice and a colorful array of vegetables.

All through dinner, Charlie kept asking Mac questions about his upcoming project at Disney Studios. Mac kept answering Charlie's questions with short replies. Linda started counting the number of words Mac was using to answer each question and then mentally deciding if his replies had actually formed an entire sentence.

"I've been retired for awhile now," Charlie told Mac. "But I wouldn't mind doing some film work again. Nothing big, mind you, a bit part would suit me just fine."

Mac nodded and smiled.

"You got any small parts in your movie for an old-timer like me?"

Mac shrugged his shoulders.

"You don't know about the roles in your own movie?" LaVerne asked, obviously impatient with the whole situation.

"I'm not sure. Been awhile since I actually read the script."

Linda smiled at Mac. He was doing better—a two-sentence answer.

Scott jumped in. "Charlie's name is a big draw at the box office. It would guarantee a hit. Just ask your guys at Disney. Everyone knows Charlie."

Mac nodded.

"Well," LaVerne said. "It was nice seeing you, Mac." She struggled to her feet. "Don't forget your hat, Charlie."

Scott followed LaVerne's lead, standing up and pulling Linda up with him. Then he ran over to the other side of the table and helped Charlie get up. The waitress hadn't delivered the dinner bill yet, but Charlie threw two hundred-dollar bills on the table.

"Call me, Mac," Charlie said, jamming his hat on his head.

Linda was trying not to giggle as the four of them retrieved their shoes and made their way out of the restaurant.

Mac was left sitting at the head of the table, staring after them.

All the way back to the beach, Charlie and LaVerne argued about whether Mac would call or not.

Scott was driving Charlie's Lincoln Continental. Linda was seated in the front with him, while Charlie and La-Verne occupied the backseat. The car was almost as long and sleek as a limousine, but instead of a conservative color, Charlie had custom-ordered it in pink.

"I'll give him till Friday, then his name comes off the luau list," Charlie said.

"I'm crossing it off tonight," LaVerne told him.

"I never met anyone so quiet before," Linda said. "I thought all producers were big talkers."

"Most of them are," Charlie said. "Big talk, little action."

"Sounds like our love life," LaVerne said.

Linda put her hand over her mouth to stifle a laugh. Scott chuckled softly, then decided to change the subject.

"Tell Linda about your luau."

"The biggest beach bash of the year," LaVerne said. "People mark their calendars a year in advance."

"How many guests do you have?" Linda asked.

"We try to keep it under two hundred," LaVerne said. "It's not easy when you've been around as long as Charlie and I. We know everyone."

"Sounds like you're going to need a lot of help. I'd be happy to pitch in."

"Thanks, kid, but we hire people to do the actual work. Of course, Charlie likes to roast the pigs himself, but everything else is done by caterers and servers."

"I don't think there's a better party this side of Hawaii," Scott added. "Real hula dancers and fire-eaters."

"When is it?" Linda asked.

"The end of next month. You think you'll still be here?" LaVerne asked Linda.

"I don't know."

"We'll make her stay," Scott said, reaching over and squeezing Linda's hand. "I need a date."

They had arrived at the Cavanaughs'. Scott pulled the car into the garage behind the house. They all piled out and went through the garage door that led to the kitchen area.

"You kids wants some hot chocolate?" LaVerne asked.

Scott glanced at the clock shaped like a huge apple on the wall over the kitchen sink. "No, thanks. It's still early. Linda and I should try to get some work done on the script."

"Write a part for me," Charlie told him.

"I'd love to," Linda said.

"Make it a small one. Charlie's too senile to learn a lot of lines," LaVerne quipped.

Scott and Linda made a hasty exit before a new argument involving Charlie's diminishing skills could begin.

Work on the script lasted until after midnight. Linda rubbed her eyes and shut down the computer for the night.

"Two hours on three pages," she said.

"But they're good pages," Scott told her. "That's what counts."

"Right." She smiled at him. "And we've left off at a good place to start tomorrow."

"You're amazing," Scott said, looking at her with a serious expression. "You really don't need my help on this at all."

"That's not true. For one thing, you're a lot more objective about this story than I am. I'm much too close to it. You're bringing a fresh perspective to the story and that's making it stronger. Besides, you know all the technical movie terms and I don't."

"Okay," Scott said. "I'll accept your accolades, if you'll take a walk on the beach with me. Did you bring a jacket?"

"No. But I've been sitting too long. I could use the exercise."

"I'll find something for you to wear. Can't have you catching cold on me."

A few minutes later, Linda and Scott were walking along the shore together. Linda was wearing one of Scott's sweatshirts. The fresh clean smells of the surf and sand mingled with the faint hint of cedar that clung to the sweatshirt. The logo on the front was almost washed away, but the letters USC were still visible.

"Did you go to USC?" Linda asked.

"No. Carla bought that for me. Come to think of it, Carla buys a lot of my clothes."

"She's a really lovely person," Linda said sincerely. "Your parents did a good job."

"I had the best."

"This really is a heavenly place," Linda said. "But . . ."

Scott pulled her to a stop and placed a finger across her lips to stop her. "No buts, not tonight," he pleaded.

"Then just tell me why a man with all your talent and charm chooses to shut himself off from the rest of the world. You could be a top screenwriter, an actor, anything you wanted to be."

"I was what I wanted to be," he told her softly. "Until I met you."

"And?"

"And you make me want to be more. Only I'm not sure I can do it."

"Why not?"

Scott guided her away from the water's edge. They had reached a deserted area of the beach, where huge boulders jutted out of the sand and formed protective barriers from the water and wind.

"Come on," Scott said, leading her into the dark shelter of a shallow cave. He plopped down on the sand and stared out at the ocean. Linda followed his lead, settling herself down next to him.

"You didn't answer my question," she prompted, after they were settled side by side, their bodies touching lightly.

Scott smiled and shrugged his broad shoulders, then he began to speak. "When I was a little kid, my dad sold life insurance. We lived in an average house, in an average neighborhood. My mom worked in the same insurance office as a secretary. During the week, Carla and I were latch-key kids, but it was okay because on weekends, mom and dad were there to play with us, and take us to all kinds of great places. We went to the zoo, the movies, the park, anything that was fun and not too expensive."

"Sounds nice," Linda said.

"It was. Then, my dad got a promotion to sales manager of his office. It meant more money, so we moved to a bigger house in a nicer neighborhood. He wasn't around as much on weekends, but it was still okay. A few years later, Dad got another promotion, then another. The houses kept getting bigger, the neighborhoods nicer. Carla and I had tons of toys and clothes, but Dad wasn't home much anymore. He was always working, traveling, making more and more money. Then, one day he came home early and took Mom, Carla, and me for a ride. He said he had a big surprise for us. The surprise was this beach house. He said this was something he had always wanted, for himself and his family, and now he could afford it. He told us that we were going to spend all our summers here. He said he and I would ride the waves together. I was so excited, not because of the beach or the beach house, but because I thought he was going to be spending more time with us. And maybe he would have, if he'd lived."

"What happened to him?" Linda asked softly.

"Two days later, he was working late at his office. He always worked late, had to with all the responsibilities of his high-paying job. He had a massive heart attack. Died right there sitting behind his desk. The cleaning crew found him. He was thirty-six years old."

"I'm sorry," Linda whispered.

"So that's my story," Scott continued. "I was twelve when he died, and I promised myself I'd never let money become that important to me. I promised myself I'd enjoy what my dad died to give me, maybe enough for both of us."

Linda reached out and touched him gently on the cheek. "I can understand how you'd feel that way," she told him.

"I hope so," Scott said, placing his hand over hers. "Because I don't want to lose whatever this is that's drawing us closer."

Linda sighed and pulled away from him. She wanted Scott to understand what drove her to achieve all the things he seemed to reject.

"My father was an invalid," she said in a rush. "He had been a construction worker. A few weeks before I was born, a pallet of bricks toppled over and crushed his legs. After I was born, my mother went to work and Dad stayed home and took care of me. I don't know how he managed in a wheelchair, but he did. Since he couldn't run or even walk with me, he had to find other ways to entertain me, so he made up stories. They were wonderful stories, so full of fun and imagination. I loved to listen to him, and even though his stories always had different settings and different characters, the lesson in them was always the same."

"And what was that?" Scott asked.

"Follow your dreams. No matter what life hands you, don't give up. Keep on trying. I guess that's why I've worked so hard to become a successful writer. I want the world to hear Dad's stories, to feel the magic they brought into my life."

"Did your dad write?"

"No. He couldn't read or write very well, but he sure could make up a terrific story. *The Magic Camera* is one of his, with some additions and revisions of my own. It has a special place in my heart because of that."

"Well," Scott said softly, placing his hands on either side of her face. "It seems you and I aren't so different after all."

"Of course we are," Linda protested. "We're like night and day."

"I'd rather think of us as sunlight and starlight," he said softly, lowering his lips to hers.

This time Linda didn't pull away. Scott's kiss was long, and slow, and sweet. Sunlight and starlight melting into a spectacular dawn of warmth and promise.

Chapter Ten

The days flew by as Scott and Linda spent every waking minute on the script. By the end of the second week, the only scene left was the troublesome one they had skipped.

As the sun set on Friday evening, Linda was running the spell check on the computer. Scott wandered into the kitchen.

"Guess what?" he called out. "We're out of food."

LaVerne sent Linda off in the mornings with coffee and pastries. Lunch and dinner were always assorted items from Scott's freezer, thawed and heated in the microwave. They had been eating regularly, but never a sit-down meal. They ate while they worked, with neither of them giving much thought to what they were consuming.

"Carla hasn't been by with care packages," Linda commented, still watching the spell check work its way through the script pages.

"I think she's afraid she'll catch us in a compromising situation," Scott said with a devilish grin.

Linda's internal thermometer went up a few degrees. She took a deep breath and decided to ignore Scott's remark.

"Do you want to drive into town with me?" Scott asked. "I'll let you push the grocery cart."

"You push the grocery cart," Linda said. "If we're going into town, I'm going to make a phone call." It had been days since Linda had received any phone messages, and she was suddenly hungry for news from New York. The spell check function ended and Linda saved the script pages. She jumped to her feet and looked at Scott, who had flopped down in a chair. "Let's go," she told him.

"Right now?"

"Yes, please."

Scott shrugged and got to his feet again. "Have you seen my wallet?" he asked.

"It's in the desk, top right-hand drawer."

"I never put it in the desk."

"No," Linda told him patiently. "You throw it on the floor. I picked it up and put it in the desk."

"Did you look through it?" His tone was teasing.

"Yes, I took all the credit cards and left the cash," she replied. "Will you hurry up?"

"I have to find the car keys."

"They're probably in the car."

"You're probably right."

Linda banged out the door and down the stairs. It was three hours later in New York, but there was a good chance Hilary would still be in her office. If not, Linda could try her at home.

"I know you are very disciplined," Scott said, as they drove away from the ocean. "So you probably finish every project you start, but this is a first for me." He reached over and patted her hand. "Thanks for letting me work with you."

"You're welcome," Linda said. "But we're not entirely finished. We still have one more scene to write, and then we have to give it to Dancer for his approval."

"Frank will be jumping up and down with happiness. This project has box-office hit written all over it."

"And what about the scene we skipped?" Linda asked.

"I'm thinking about a solution to that," Scott told her. "By the time we get home, I'll have it figured out."

Linda couldn't help but smile at his newfound confidence. "Okay," she replied cheerfully. "Then I'll quit worrying about it."

When they pulled into the parking lot of the shopping center, Linda looked around for a telephone.

"There's one in the drug store," Scott told her. "How many hours will you need?"

"Very funny. You start the shopping, I'll catch up with you in a few minutes."

As Linda had suspected, Hilary was still in her office. "I'm so glad you called," she told Linda. "I miss you, but I didn't want to call and interrupt work on the script. How is it going?"

"It's almost done. What's going on there?"

"Do you want the truth or unsubstantiated gossip?"

"Both."

Hilary laughed and gave Linda a rundown on mutual friends and the latest theater news. Then Linda told her about life at the beach and the Crazy Cavanaughs.

"They've been so great. When I get home I'll have to send them a really spectacular gift."

"You haven't said a word about your co-writer—Scott, isn't it?"

"Scott," Linda affirmed. "He's actually very talented and I've really enjoyed working with him."

"And?"

"And we're in town getting groceries, so I'd better get off the phone and help him."

"How domestic," Hilary said. "Is there a chance you two could become more than co-writers?"

"I don't know," Linda answered honestly.

"Well, there's not much going on here right now. Why don't you take some time off and find out for sure?"

"Maybe I will."

The phone call ended and Linda went into the grocery store to search for Scott. She found him in the produce section balancing a honeydew melon in each hand and looking from one to the other like he was making a life-changing decision. Linda walked up next to him. He turned and smiled his perfect smile. "Hey, you're the other half of this team. Which one do you like?"

"Both of them." She grabbed them out of his hands and placed them in the cart.

"You look happy," Scott commented. "Good news from New York?"

"Not really, just news in general, but it made me feel connected again. Now, what did you buy for dinner?"

"They have some good-looking roasted chickens in the deli."

"You finish up here. I'll get the chickens," Linda offered. "Just point me in the right direction."

Linda went to the deli section and had them pack up two whole chickens, a quart of potato salad, a pint of cole slaw, pasta salad, and corn muffins.

Scott was already loading the other groceries into the car when she met him with her dinner purchases. He looked at her and grinned. "I figured it out," he said, helping her into the car.

"Figured what out?"

"How to draft the missing scene. I'll tell you when we get home, while we eat dinner."

When we get home. He said the phrase so naturally, like the beach was her home as much as his.

The night was warm, so they had dinner up on the deck. Linda watched the sun melt away, turning the clouds pink, orange, and finally purple. Although her conversation with Hilary had made her feel reconnected to New York and the theater scene there, Linda had to admit that she had also formed an emotional attachment the beach.

The big question was whether it was the hospitality of the Cavanaughs, the beauty and tranquility of the beach, or the chemistry between her and Scott that made her feel that way. Maybe it was all three.

Chapter Eleven

Charlie and LaVerne were sitting on their patio listening to Doris Day sing "My Secret Love." It was close to 10:00 P.M. and the air was still balmy. A full moon shimmered down on the ocean as it sent gentle, quiet waves to cover the shore, leaving it wet and glistening.

"We did it!" Scott yelled as soon as he and Linda were in shouting distance of the elderly couple.

"It's about time," Charlie shouted back. "Pretty girls like Linda don't grow on trees, you know. When's the wedding?"

Linda was hugging a copy of the script to her chest. It was all neatly printed and securely fastened into a binder she had made from a file folder. She held the script in the air and waved it at them.

LaVerne jumped to her feet. "The script, you old fool," she said to Charlie. "The kids have finished the script!"

Scott and Linda bounded onto the patio and LaVerne hugged them both. Charlie stood up and scowled at them.

"There's a part in it for you, Charlie," Linda said, thrusting the script at him. "Lyle. It starts on page twenty-two."

Charlie grabbed the script and ran into the house.

"Can't see a dang thing without his glasses," LaVerne explained. "This calls for a celebration. Come on inside. I've got apple pie."

74

In the last two weeks, Linda had learned that LaVerne's expertise in the kitchen was limited to two things: hot chocolate and apple pie. Both were made from scratch and both were rich and delicious.

LaVerne had grown up on a farm in Michigan, where the apple orchard provided her family's main source of income. "My mother baked apple pies every day of her life. It's a family tradition," LaVerne had told Linda more than once.

Scott and Linda sat next to each other at the round wooden table. Cloth placemats with bright red apples were placed in front of them. Linda gazed around at the kitchen that LaVerne had decorated with an apple motif, her way of displaying her roots to all who entered.

LaVerne was bustling around, making coffee and clattering china. Linda breathed in the wonderful scent of cinnamon and apples and looked anxiously towards the doorway. Charlie had not reappeared with the script. He had taken it into his den and closed the door.

Scott reached over and placed his hand over hers. "Don't worry," he whispered in her ear. "He'll love it."

Linda turned and looked at Scott. He looked as excited as a kid on Christmas morning. "It *is* good, isn't it?"

"This is the best script I have ever read," Charlie announced, suddenly appearing in the doorway. He walked over and slammed the script on the table in front of Scott and Linda. "It's got everything: comedy, romance, baseball, and a dashing older character who will steal the film."

Scott and Linda both burst out laughing.

"Charlie, you've only been in the den for ten minutes," Linda said. "You couldn't possibly have read the entire script."

"You ever hear of Evelyn Woods's speed-reading school? I was her top student."

LaVerne walked over and pushed Charlie into the nearest chair. "Calm down, honey," she said. "That must be some great character these kids wrote for you."

"Are you sure Frank will give me the part?" Charlie asked.

"I already asked him," Scott replied. "It's in the bag, so you don't have to butter us up anymore."

"Okay. So I only read the lines you wrote for Lyle, but that's all I needed to read to know you kids have got a real winner here." He stabbed his finger on the cover of the script.

"Linda gets the credit for that," Scott said. "She's the beauty and the brains of this duo."

"Scott is being too generous," Linda said quickly. "He's really quite brilliant. He came up with the idea that enabled us to finish the script tonight."

"Now I get time off for good behavior," Scott added, winking at Linda. "And I'm hoping we can convince Linda to stay around and see what life on the beach is really like."

"I really should be getting back to New York," Linda said.

LaVerne turned from the counter where she was cutting generous slices of apple pie and shook her head firmly. "Linda, there's no way I'm letting you leave before the luau. I already ordered your grass skirt."

Charlie whooped his approval. Linda extracted her hand from Scott's grasp and got up to help LaVerne serve the pie and coffee.

"To your success," LaVerne said, holding her coffee cup in the air.

It reminded Linda of Hilary's toast at her going-away party. She had come to Hollywood with high expectations for her career. Those expectations had all come crashing down the day she met Scott Richards. Now, as she raised her own cup and looked around the table, she realized that the weeks she had spent at the beach working with Scott and getting to know the Cavanaughs had filled her with a new set of expectations that had nothing to do with furthering her career.

Later, when she walked Scott out to the patio, she voiced her feelings. "I came to the beach filled with uncertainty, but working with you and living with Charlie and LaVerne has turned out to be one of the best experiences of my life. Knowing you has changed me, made me realize that I need to slow down and stop letting my whole life revolve around my work."

"Does that mean you're going to stick around for awhile?"

"I'm thinking about it."

Scott drew her into his arms and kissed the top of her head. "I don't want you to leave me," he whispered.

At that moment, Linda felt like she could stay there in his arms forever. She raised her face and welcomed his kiss, and the peaceful night exploded into a sensation of joy and longing. Scott slowly pulled back and smiled at her, and Linda suddenly felt very frightened and vulnerable.

"I don't know if I can do this, Scott," Linda said, pushing herself away from him. "We have to keep things light and uncomplicated."

"A platonic relationship?"

"Yes."

"I think we already have that."

"We do, and it has to stay that way. Your charm and appeal are overwhelming, but we're too different, and I'm not at all sure we can resolve those differences over the long term."

"Okay, so stay here for awhile and we'll see if we can work it out."

Linda sighed and forced a smile. "I'll see you tomorrow."

"Right. Tomorrow we deliver your script to Frank."

"Our script."

"Our script," Scott agreed. He kissed her lightly on the cheek and turned her towards the house. "You'd better get inside."

Linda nodded and moved away from him towards the sliding glass door at the back of the patio. She stopped there and watched Scott walk away. He disappeared into the night.

Inside the house, LaVerne was waiting for her. "Sit down, kiddo. I'm going to give you some advice."

Linda smiled and sat down obediently on the edge of the sofa where LaVerne was sitting with her arms folded across her chest.

"I know you're used to those high-powered, over-achievers in New York, but you're never going to find another man as good as Scott," LaVerne said. "You can stay here as long as you want. We love having you, and you owe it to yourself to stick around and find out if you and Scott can make it work. I'm betting you can."

Linda nodded. "I talked to my agent on the phone earlier. She said there's not much happening in New York right now."

"Good. Then it's settled."

"I'll stay for the luau," Linda said. "But I'm not wearing a grass skirt."

"We'll get you a dress with big flowers instead."

"And you have to let me help you and Charlie with the party."

"You can help me. Charlie is beyond help."

Chapter Twelve

Scott and Linda delivered the movie script to Dancer Productions the next morning. Frank promised to read it right away and get it over to the director he wanted.

"I'm staying with the Cavanaughs for a while longer," Linda told him. "So if you need any changes in the script . . ."

"You'll be out of luck," Scott interrupted. "Linda is officially on vacation and we're going to Disneyland."

"I get the message," Frank said. "Go have fun. You deserve it."

Linda was so entranced by Disneyland, she and Scott spent two days there. They went on all the rides, saw all the shows, stuffed themselves with food, and had silly photos taken with the costumed characters.

Since it was summertime, the park was filled with children of all ages. Linda especially liked watching the look of wonder on the young faces, and knew that her own face probably bore the same expression. She bought souvenirs for Hilary and some of her other New York friends.

Other days were spent at other tourist spots like Universal Studios and Knott's Berry Farm. Nights at the beach were spent swimming, walking along the shore, and playing cards with Charlie and LaVerne.

Word came that the director liked the script and had put it on his shooting schedule.

"And you were worried," Scott told Linda, after LaVerne gave them the phone message.

"Actually," Linda admitted, "I've been having too much fun to be worried about anything."

"Okay. I was worried for you. And I think that's a first for me."

"That's really sweet."

"It is, isn't it?" Scott replied with an impish grin.

With each passing day, Scott and Linda drew closer and became more aware of their feelings for each other. Phone calls to and from New York diminished in importance. All of Linda's energy and emotions were focused on Scott and the magic of their relationship. They were like teenagers falling in love for the first time, as enamored of the process as they were with each other.

"One of these nights, we're going to have to sit down and have a very serious talk," Scott told Linda at the end of the second week.

"I know," Linda said. "But not tonight. We have a big meeting tomorrow and I need to focus on that."

"Frank loves the script; the director loves the script. This meeting is just a formality."

"That's what *you* say. I don't think it's going to be that simple."

Scott made a face at her. "Oh, I get it. You think I'm going to screw up."

"No, Scott. I'm afraid *I'm* going to screw up."

Scott laughed and pulled her into a bear hug. "Honey, one look at your big brown eyes and Templeton will be jumping through hoops to impress you. He's a skirt chaser of the highest order."

An image of Rick Ralston flashed through Linda's mind. "You'd better be kidding," Linda warned. "I hate men like that."

"You'll like Templeton," Scott insisted. "Because he is

an excellent director and he will make your movie a box-office hit."

"Our movie," Linda corrected.

Scott laughed and held her at arm's length. "Okay, our movie."

As it turned out, Scott was right about the meeting. They had a lovely lunch on Frank Dancer's patio and discussed casting and scheduling. Preproduction had already begun, but the actual shooting wouldn't start for at least six weeks.

"Will you still be here, Linda?" Bob Templeton asked.

"I'm not sure," she answered, avoiding Scott's eyes.

"Well, the script is in great shape, so I'm sure any changes will be minor ones. Scott can take care of anything that's needed and keep you informed. With fax machines and e-mail, New York and Los Angeles are a lot closer than they used to be."

"Faxes and e-mails will never take the place of face-to-face communications," Scott said pointedly.

On the way back to the beach, Scott reminded Linda of the serious talk they were supposed to have.

"After the luau," Linda promised.

"I have some important questions for you," Scott told her.

"And I have some for you," Linda countered.

Chapter Thirteen

The day of the luau dawned bright and clear and the atmosphere at Charlie and LaVerne's was charged with excitement.

At 1:00 that afternoon an army of professionals moved in and started transforming the house, patio, and beach area into Hawaii. By four, the pigs were turning slowly over glowing coals in pits that had been scooped out of the sand. An expert catering staff dressed in proper island garb moved through the early arrivals serving exotic drinks.

LaVerne had insisted that she and Linda wear matching dresses and had had the garments custom-made. Linda felt like a Hawaiian princess in the long, flowing dress fashioned out of fabric as light and airy as cotton candy. A white background was splashed with hundreds of small, bright-colored flowers.

Linda and LaVerne greeted guests with leis fashioned out of the same flowers that adorned their dresses. Scott and Charlie were on the beach supervising the roasting chores. Both men were dressed in white cutoffs with shirts that matched LaVerne and Linda's dresses.

Linda had expected to see Frank and Carla Dancer, but Scott told her that they were out of town on business.

By the time the authentic Hawaiian buffet was served,

the number of party guests had swelled to over two hundred. Everywhere Linda looked she saw a famous face.

"I feel like I'm actually in Hawaii," Linda told Scott.

"With all these actors and producers here, it's more like a movie spectacle set in Hawaii," Scott replied.

They were standing on the beach watching as the catering crew moved through the crowd picking up the remains of the buffet dinner.

"I'm really glad I stayed for this," Linda said.

Scott put his arm around her shoulder. "So am I. You know, I've never had a girl for a buddy before. It's really nice."

Linda laughed. "Is this your lead-in for our serious talk?"

Scott tilted her chin up and kissed her. "No. Too many people around. And before you jump to any wrong conclusions, I enjoy having you as a friend, but I want a lot more."

The flaming torches positioned around the area seemed to dance in Scott's eyes. "So do I," she admitted softly.

"Well, at least we're in agreement on that point."

Just then, Charlie pushed his way towards them. "Hey, what are you doing way over here?"

"Just talking," Scott said.

"Well, I'm stealing your girl. Lots of people she needs to meet. She can talk to you tomorrow."

Scott waved as Charlie dragged her off. For the next hour, she let Charlie lead her around like a puppy on a leash. "This is Linda, she's a wonderful new screenwriter. Doing a film for Frank Dancer right now, and if you're smart you'll remember her name. Talent like hers doesn't grow on trees, you know."

The evening was like none other. Even the premiere night's extravaganza at Dancer's house paled in comparison. Linda met so many people, so many powerful Hollywood icons, she began to lose a grip on reality. Everyone was so charming, and thanks to Charlie's buildup, they all wanted to read anything she cared to send them or they wanted to set up a meeting while she was in town. "Have your agent give me a call," she heard over and over again.

Soon her hands were crammed with business cards, many with private, unlisted phone numbers scribbled on them.

Linda was totally overwhelmed and wanted desperately to run to a telephone and call Hilary in New York, but a gong was sounding.

Scott came up beside her. "That's the signal that the entertainment is about to begin."

"Oh, my God," Linda whispered back. "I can't believe this. Everyone I met wants to have lunch with me."

Scott grinned and kissed her on the cheek. "I'd like to have you for lunch," he said.

A shiver like an electric current ran through Linda's body. She stiffened and pulled away from him. "Don't try to distract me," she warned.

"Yes, ma'am," he replied curtly. "Am I allowed to sit with you during the show?"

Scott extended a muscular arm and Linda placed her hand lightly on top of it. Together they made their way towards the patio area where people were gathering for the show.

Not to be outdone by the decorations and food, the performers put on a spectacular show. Singers, Hawaiian dancers, and a fire-eater had the crowd cheering their approval.

By midnight, most of the guests had left. The few who remained were inside the house chatting with Charlie and LaVerne. Scott and Linda were on the patio. The last of the staff members had driven off a few minutes earlier.

There was a cloudless sky overhead providing the perfect backdrop for millions of twinkling stars. With Scott's strong arm around her, Linda gazed up and marveled at the spectacular sight.

"Almost takes your breath away, doesn't it?" Scott asked.

"I think I'm beginning to understand why you live out here," Linda answered.

Scott drew her closer and she allowed herself the pleasure of leaning back against the rock hardness of his chest.

"Thank goodness I don't have to drive anywhere," she mused.

"Just what I was thinking," Scott murmured, his lips grazing the top of her ear.

Linda summoned enough strength to pull free of Scott and the sparks of desire his lips were igniting.

"Hey, you two," Charlie called from the doorway. "The party's still going on in here. Come on inside."

"Get lost, Charlie," Scott said affectionately.

"Thank you for introducing me to all your friends," Linda said.

"Friends!" Charlie snorted, interrupting her. "Those people aren't friends. They're barracudas. And if you want to survive in this business, young lady, you'd better learn to tell the difference." Then, to soften his rebuke, he added, "Just let me know who you're interested in working with, and I'll tell you whether they can be trusted or not."

Linda walked over and planted a light kiss on Charlie's wrinkled, leathery cheek. "Thanks, Charlie. You're the best."

"I love you too," Scott said. "Now will you please get lost?"

Charlie shook his head and closed the door, leaving them alone again.

"I think tonight is going to be a turning point in my career," Linda said, twirling around in her gossamer dress.

"If that's what you want," Scott replied. "Just keep in mind, a lot of those people won't remember who you are tomorrow."

The smile faded from Linda's face, and, like Charlie, Scott tried to soften his remark. "Sorry, honey. But this is Hollywood, the town where promises are made to be broken, along with dreams and hearts."

"And how many hearts have you broken?" Linda countered, surprising him with her cynical tone.

"I'm not going to break yours," Scott said easily. He moved forward and placed his hands on her shoulders, forcing her to look into his eyes. "But I have the feeling you may break mine."

"I might," Linda agreed, sliding her arms around his neck. "Into a million tiny pieces."

Still feeling both giddy and bold from the events of the evening, Linda pulled his head down and kissed him on the mouth.

His powerful arms closed around her as the kiss grew more searching and passionate. Linda leaned into him, aching for his touch. Scott turned her away from the ocean, shielding her body from the prickly spray of the surf, as his hands began to move down her back in a slow, tantalizing motion.

Then, all at once, he stopped kissing her. His hands took hold of her arms and gently lowered them away from him. "I think it's time we had that talk," he said softly.

Linda nodded and let him lead her off the patio, out onto the beach. They settled down in the sand.

"Let me start," Linda said. "I know you think that meeting all these producers tonight is fueling my ambitions, and it is, but it is also making me think that I can stay here and work. Let's face it. Movie work pays a lot better than stage work. Even if you get to Broadway, which is still a cherished dream of mine, you don't earn the kind of money you can earn in Hollywood."

"Are you offering to support me?" Scott teased.

Linda laughed. "No. Not at all. I'm saying that we could compromise. I could stay here at the beach with you and we could work here together."

"How about if you work and I watch?"

"Scott, I'm trying to have a serious discussion about our future. Maybe I should have let you go first. It seems we have different ideas of what our future should be."

"I just want you to be a part of my life, to love you, to make you happy. If you need to work to be happy, then I'll support your efforts, but don't expect me to find the same joy in work that you do. I don't have the talent or the heart for it."

"You do have the talent, Scott," Linda said firmly.

"Maybe I do, but that's not the real issue here. The big question is, can you accept me as I am?"

Linda took a deep breath. "I think I already have."

"Linda! Linda!" LaVerne was shouting at her from the patio.

Scott stood up and pulled Linda to her feet. "Your chaperone is calling you," he said. "How about if we continue this talk over dinner tomorrow night? I'll take you into town, someplace swanky."

"No," Linda replied. "Let's have a quiet dinner on the deck. I'll bet LaVerne will let us have some of her leftovers."

"No leftovers. I have to take my car into town to be serviced. I'll pick up dinner for us."

By the time they got to the patio, LaVerne had disappeared inside the house again.

Scott kissed Linda lightly on the lips. "I'll come down and get you tomorrow evening, around six. Prepare yourself for another big question."

Before Linda could reply, Scott took off running. She stared after him, her heart pounding as hard as Scott's footsteps in the sand.

LaVerne was waiting inside the door for her again.

"You two looked mighty cozy down there," she said, with a sly smile. "Sorry to break it up, but your agent called."

"Hilary?"

"Right. Of course no one was in the house to answer the phone, so she left a message on the machine. I just listened to it. She wants you to call her back as soon as possible."

Linda glanced at the clock on the wall. It was after midnight. With daylight saving time in effect, it was three hours later in New York.

"It's almost three A.M. in New York," Linda said. "I'll call her first thing in the morning."

"Oh, heck, I forgot about the time difference. Dragged

you off the beach for nothing. Did I interrupt something important?"

"It's okay, LaVerne. It's late and we're all tired. Scott and I can finish our talk tomorrow."

"How are you and Scott?"

"We're good," Linda told her. "I think we're going to be just fine."

Tears suddenly appeared in LaVerne's eyes. "That's what I was hoping you'd say. I'd like nothing better than to see you two get together permanently."

"If we do, we owe it all to you and Charlie and your generosity."

"Our pleasure," LaVerne assured her. "Well, we best be getting some sleep. Charlie's already in there sawing logs. I'll have to find my earplugs or sleep in the other guest room."

Linda laughed and gave the older woman a hug. "Thanks, LaVerne. It was a wonderful party, the best I've ever attended."

"Next year will be even better," LaVerne said.

Linda fell asleep thinking about LaVerne's last statement. So far this year had been pretty spectacular, but with Scott at her side, next year could be even better.

Chapter Fourteen

Linda set her alarm and got up at 7:00 the next morning. She showered and dressed quickly, then fixed coffee and carried a cup into Charlie's den and closed the door so as not to disturb the Cavanaughs.

Charlie and LaVerne were still sleeping, which was unusual for them. They were probably worn out from the luau.

It was already after 10:00 in New York. She dialed the number for her agent's office. Hilary snatched up the phone on the first ring.

"Hi, Hilary, it's Linda."

"Praise the Lord," Hilary exclaimed. "I thought I was going to have to send out the National Guard. Where have you been?"

"There was a huge party here last night, a luau. No one was manning the telephone so I didn't get your message until after midnight. So how are things in New York?"

"Things in New York are incredible, Linda. For you, things in New York could not be better, unless of course you were here in New York."

"What's happened?"

"Are you sitting down?"

"Yes. Tell me," Linda cried.

"The Magic Camera is going to Broadway with—" Hilary,

also very dramatic, paused for effect—"the Solomon Organization."

"Solomon?" Linda couldn't believe her ears. Solomon was one of the biggest producers in the world. "But they usually do musicals."

"Yes, they do," Hilary agreed. "And *The Magic Camera* is going to be a musical."

Linda felt her heart skip a beat. She had a million questions, but couldn't utter even one.

"Here's the short version," Hilary said. "I met Ken Hartman at a party last weekend. Since his last hit, everyone in town is after him to write music for their show, but he told me he couldn't find a project he could get excited about. Then he started talking about this wonderful play he saw last year and how he thought he could write some dynamite music for it."

"My play!" Linda squealed. "He was talking about my play?"

"You got it, kid. As soon as he started telling me about it, I got goose bumps. The next morning, we went to Solomon, and they practically fell at his feet. The contracts are signed by everyone but you."

"Oh, Hilary," Linda whispered. "I think I may cry."

"Don't you want to know how much money they're giving you first?"

"No. Just tell them I said yes."

"I did that two hours ago. When I didn't hear from you, I was afraid to wait any longer. Now they want to know when you're coming back here to work on the show."

Linda suddenly remembered Scott and their date that evening. "Oh, wow. I'm not sure."

"Hartman wants to meet with you tomorrow to discuss his song ideas. Can you fly back today?"

"Okay," Linda said, getting control of her thoughts. "Fax the contract to Frank Dancer's office this morning. I'll go there, sign it, and fax it right back. I'll call you from there."

Linda and Hilary spent a few more minutes finalizing plans for the morning. Linda hung up the phone and stared into space, stunned by her good fortune. Ken Hartman was considered a musical genius. Having him write music for her play pretty much guaranteed a long Broadway run.

Linda hurried out of the house and started down the beach towards Scott's house. She had to talk to him right away. Her heart fell to her feet when she realized that Scott's car was gone. "Darn him," she whispered. "He never gets up and out this early."

Just to be sure, she went up the back stairs and pounded on the door. It swung open, and a quick look inside confirmed the fact that Scott was indeed gone.

Linda sprinted back down the beach and into the Cavanaughs' house once more. She heard dishes rattling in the kitchen and found Charlie there banging around in the cabinets. He was still wearing his pajamas.

"Charlie, I need a big favor."

"Help me find some aspirin and I'll promise you anything."

Linda ran into the nearest bathroom and came back with a bottle of aspirin. Charlie had thrown himself into a chair. She filled a glass with water and set it and the aspirin on the table in front of Charlie.

While Charlie shook out two pills and swallowed them down with the water, Linda told him her news. "I have to go back to New York right away. Scott is gone already and I need someone to drive me to Frank Dancer's office. My agent is faxing the contract there."

Charlie nodded thoughtfully, as if he were trying to comprehend what she was telling him. Then, Linda heard a car door slam and saw Scott's blond curls pass by the kitchen window.

In the next instant, Scott was knocking on the kitchen door. Linda ran to open it. Scott held out a white bakery box.

"Hi, sweetie," he said cheerfully. "I drove over to the new bakery and got some pastries. Didn't think LaVerne would be up to fixing breakfast this morning."

Linda stared at him and backed away. Suddenly the impact that her news would have on their relationship seemed daunting.

Charlie got up and started out of the kitchen. "I'll get LaVerne. Hope you got cheese danish; it's her favorite."

"I did," Scott called after him. Scott set the box on the table and put his arms around Linda. "Nice of him to leave us alone for a minute."

"I was looking for you. I need to talk to you."

"You look upset." Scott let go of Linda and backed away. "What's wrong?"

"Nothing's wrong," Linda assured him. "Just the opposite, actually. I talked to my agent, and she gave me some good news about one of my plays," Linda said carefully. "The one you saw, about the magic camera. Another producer is interested in it."

"Well that's great, honey. Congratulations."

"Thanks. I have to go to Frank's office this morning. She's going to fax me a contract to look over and then I have to fly back to New York."

"How soon?"

"Today. The producer is the Solomon Organization. They want me back in New York right away."

"Well, that sounds very good for you and your play, and very bad for me and the beach," Scott said. The smile was gone from his face and his voice was low and tight.

He was upset and angry and it gave Linda a jolt. "I'm really sorry, Scott, but I have to go. This is big-time, this is Broadway, and the best part is that Ken Hartman is going to write music for the show. That pretty much guarantees a hit."

"Well, that's even better for you."

Linda rushed forward and put her arms around his neck. "Please don't be upset with me. I have to do this. The play will have to be rewritten to accommodate the music, and I have to be there to collaborate with the composer."

Scott pulled her close. "I understand that. What I don't understand is why you have to leave today."

Linda felt tears sting her eyes. She leaned against him,

breathing in the fresh scent of the ocean that always ema-
nated from him. "The composer wants to meet with me
tomorrow. I promised Hilary . . . " Linda let her voice trail
off and Scott took her by the shoulders and held her away
from him. Linda looked into his eyes and saw the disappointment there. "I have to pack," she said. Scott nodded
and let her go.

She ran down the hallway. As she got to her room, she
could hear LaVerne and Charlie making a noisy entrance
into the kitchen.

"You'd better not be lying about that cheese danish,"
LaVerne yelled.

Linda closed the door to her room and leaned against it.
Saying good-bye to Charlie and LaVerne was going to be
hard. Saying good-bye to Scott was going to be even worse.

Linda thought maybe LaVerne would bound down the
hall to hear the story firsthand, but no one came near her
room. She was packed and ready to go within an hour.
Charlie and LaVerne were genuinely happy for her, and
that made it possible for them to get through their good-
byes without too many tears.

"Now you call me as soon as you get settled in again,"
LaVerne instructed. "And if anyone gives you trouble, you
call me and I'll come running. And don't forget to send us
tickets to the show when it opens."

"Front row, center," Linda promised.

Scott made no comment as he loaded her luggage into
the car and they sped off to the coastal highway. The morning air was unseasonably cool, and Scott had the top up.
The silence in the car was like a sudden frost, chilly and
uncomfortable.

"Scott, you know this is a dream come true for me. And
you know that my professional life sometimes has to take
precedence over my personal life."

"Maybe you can't really separate them," Scott said.

"Maybe I can't," Linda agreed. *And maybe I should have
kept a safe distance from you,* Linda thought, hurt by
Scott's remark.

Scott reached over and flipped on the radio. Nothing else was said until they reached the parking lot behind Dancer's office building. Scott got out of the car and came around and opened the door for Linda.

"I'll leave your luggage with the doorman in the lobby," Scott told her.

Linda was stunned. "You're not coming up with me?"

"No. I've got something important I have to do. I'll try to be back in time to drive you to the airport."

Scott brushed his lips across hers in a casual light kiss and walked off, leaving her standing there, staring after him.

If she'd had the time, Linda would have cried, but it was after noon, which meant it was late afternoon in New York. With purposeful strides, Linda hurried into the office building that housed Dancer Productions.

As she pushed her way through the glass door, Julie, the receptionist, and Frank Dancer himself rushed up to greet her.

"Linda, congratulations on the Broadway deal," Dancer said enthusiastically. "We're delighted for you."

Linda was a little puzzled. "How did you know?"

"Your agent and a very nice man who said he's your composer have been calling for the past hour," Julie told her. "And your contract has already been faxed from New York."

"You can use the conference room to make your calls," Frank said, ushering Linda towards a closed door. "You'll have complete privacy." Then, turning to Julie, he added, "Julie, get Linda some coffee and bring her contract into the conference room so she can read it undisturbed."

Julie sprang into action as Frank opened the door to the conference room. It was small with a round glass-topped table surrounded by comfortable-looking plush chairs.

"This is very nice of you," Linda said.

"Nonsense. I'm really elated for you, and the publicity this will generate will be great for the movie."

"The movie?" Linda said, feeling off-balance. "Oh, the movie, of course. I'm just a little rattled."

Julie hurried in with a steaming coffee mug that said Dancer Productions and a folder containing Linda's contract.

"Thank you," Linda murmured again.

"Take all the time you need. The phone is right there. And don't worry about the cost, it's on me. The least I can do for you."

Linda smiled and nodded. It wasn't until Frank Dancer and his secretary had both left the room that Linda realized he hadn't even asked about Scott.

Of course, Scott's relatives were used to his unpredictability. She was a novice when it came to dealing with Scott and his whims. The bond between them was still new and fragile. Linda was afraid that their relationship would not survive her success, and she was surprised to realize how much that would hurt her.

Before she could dwell on it further, Julie opened the door and popped her head inside the room. "Your agent is on line one."

Linda took a deep breath and reached for the phone. The events that would shape her life were already in progress. It was too late to change anything. "Hi, Hilary," she said, forcing cheerfulness into her tone.

"Ken Hartman is here. He wants to talk to you. And did you look at the contract yet?"

"No. I just got here. It's a long ride from the beach."

"I've got you booked on a four o'clock flight. Can you make that?"

"I think so; the airport is fairly close to the office here," Linda answered.

"Great. Here's Ken."

Linda sat down and opened the folder with the contract. Ken Hartman's voice greeted her with warmth. "Linda, I'm so happy to be working with you. Can't wait to meet you in person."

"Same here," Linda told him.

Linda and the composer talked for about twenty minutes. He was bursting with song ideas for her play, and all of them sounded wonderful. In a very good bass voice, Ken gave Linda a quick rendition of the song he was already working on. The lyrics were delightful and the tune lively. By the time the conversation ended, Linda was brimming with excitement again.

Her excitement waned when Hilary got back on the line. "You'll get to La Guardia about ten, and I'll be there to meet you."

Linda glanced at the ornate clock on the wall in the conference room. With all the new security procedures, she would have to leave for the airport in a few minutes. She was hoping to see Scott again, to try to talk to him about their relationship and see how they could make it work.

"That's fine," Linda heard herself saying. "I'll have to get going now. I'll read the contract on the plane."

"Okay, see you tonight," Hilary said.

The line clicked off and Linda slowly placed the receiver back in its cradle. Then she walked out to Julie's desk and asked her to call a cab for her.

"No problem," Julie assured her.

Frank Dancer came out of his office again. She told him to tell Scott she hadn't been able to wait for him any longer.

"Where is he?" Dancer asked, as if he had just realized his brother-in-law was missing.

"I don't know. He dropped me off and said he had to take care of some things."

"Your cab will be downstairs in two minutes," Julie called out.

Linda looked at Dancer. "I'm going back to New York right away."

"That is fast," Dancer agreed. "I was hoping to have you talk to my public relations person before you left, but it's okay. I'll have him call you in New York."

"Fine. Thanks again for everything, and say good-bye to Carla for me."

"I will," Dancer said, giving her a quick hug. "You have a safe trip home."

"If you need revisions on the script . . ." Linda began.

"I'm sure they'll be minor, and Scott can handle them. You two will be touch anyway, won't you?"

"Sure," Linda replied, not sure at all if they would be.

The cab driver loaded Linda's luggage into the cab and they took off for the airport. She would arrive at LAX in plenty of time to check in and clear security. She would even have time to get something to eat.

She didn't know where Scott was. She had been hoping he would show up before she left, but he didn't. As the taxi sped along towards the freeway, Linda gazed out the window at the ocean. The morning mist had burned off and the sun's rays danced across the water.

Memories of the last few weeks burned in Linda's mind, filling her with a sense of loss. No matter how successful her play became, would it be enough to make up for losing Scott? Would she end up regretting her decision to leave so quickly and resenting the success that took her across the country, away from Scott?

I should have told Hilary I couldn't come home yet, Linda chastised herself. A few more days couldn't have made that much difference to the producer or Hartman, but it might have made a difference to Scott. A little more time together might have . . .

Linda turned away from the window and the sparkling water that reminded her of Scott. *This is stupid,* she thought, angry with herself and with Scott. *If he cared,* he *wouldn't have dumped me off at Dancer's office like a bag of laundry.*

The cab made its way onto the freeway where the traffic was lighter than usual. They arrived at the airport a few minutes before 2:00.

The cabdriver carried Linda's luggage to the skycap's station. She paid the driver and gave him a generous tip.

Linda had a salad at a busy, noisy airport restaurant. She ate mechanically, not really tasting the food. She had some time before she had to report to her gate. She could call Dancer's office and see if Scott was there.

With that decided, Linda paid her lunch bill and found a phone removed from the flow of passengers hurrying back and forth between the departure gates. She dialed Dancer's office, and Julie answered the phone.

"Hi, Julie," Linda said in a casual tone. "I was wondering if Scott ever showed up there."

"I'm not sure," the perky secretary replied. "I've been at lunch and running errands for Mr. Dancer. Let me buzz you through to him."

Dancer came on the line. "Did Scott show up?" she asked.

"Oh yeah, showed up a little while ago. I explained about you having to leave and he took off in a hurry."

"Where did he go?"

"I don't know, but then I stopped trying to keep track of Scott a long time ago. Did you want me to give him a message for you?"

"Yes . . . I mean no . . . just tell him to call me in New York. You have my number."

"Sure thing. Oh, and I talked to my publicity guy; he'll call you in a few days for a phone interview," Dancer said.

She hung up and began walking towards the gate. She was already checked in and had her boarding pass. There was no real hurry, but Linda now felt anxious to get on the plane and fly away from California. Scott obviously didn't care that she was leaving, so the faster she put him and the beach behind her the better.

"Linda Lucas, report to the first-floor information desk please. Miss Linda Lucas, please report to the information desk on the first floor."

Linda hurried back through the checkpoint and took the escalator down to the ground floor of the airport. There she found herself facing a huge bouquet of yellow roses.

Behind the flowers was Scott. Linda was so surprised to see him she let out a small scream.

"I hope that means you're happy to see me," Scott said, handing her the flowers.

"Where did you take off to?" Linda asked. "I thought you deserted me."

"That's funny. I was thinking the same thing about you."

"I'm not deserting you, Scott. I have to do this."

"I know that. I'm not happy about it, but I do understand how much this particular play means to you, so I decided to stop pouting and get you these flowers. When I got back, Frank said you were going back to New York right away, so I called your agent and got your flight information so I could see you before you left."

"Oh, Scott." Linda pressed the roses to her face. Her eyes were filling with tears. "That was so sweet."

"Watch out for the thorns," Scott warned. "Oh, and I got you something else too. Actually, this is what took so long. I hope you like it."

He held out a small square box. Linda set the flowers down on a vacant chair and took the box. She lifted the lid and stared at Scott's gift to her. Suspended from a delicate gold chain was a small, perfectly round diamond surrounded by a circle of tiny gold stars.

"The sun and stars," Linda whispered.

Scott took the necklace from the box and fastened it around Linda's neck. Then he drew her into his arms and kissed her. "I wanted you to have something to take with you," Scott said softly in her ear. "So you don't forget me."

"I could never forget you," Linda promised.

"Even when you're the toast of Broadway?"

Linda answered him with another kiss that was interrupted by the pre-boarding announcement for Linda's flight.

"I wish you were coming with me," Linda said.

"I wish you were staying here," Scott replied.

"What are we going to do?" Linda asked.

"You are going to get on that plane and go to New York. I'm going to go back to the beach and miss you like crazy."

"Get a telephone," Linda told him. "Then at least I can talk to you every day."

"I won't be home. Frank is going to start shooting the movie next week. I'll have to be on the set every day. I'll call you from there."

"Oh, no, the movie! I should be on the set too."

"You should be there instead of me, but I'll do my best to cover for you. With any luck, the movie will wrap about the same time your play hits Broadway. Send me tickets for opening night. I'll see you, hopefully, in about two months? That is, if I don't cave and visit you earlier," he smiled.

"I hope you do . . . two months suddenly seems like a long time," Linda said.

"I know."

The second boarding call came over the loudspeaker. "Don't say good-bye," Scott cautioned, favoring her with a small smile. "I don't want all these people to see me cry."

Linda was already crying, but pulled herself together and went through security again. They checked the flowers and her purse and let her pass through to the gate.

Clutching the roses to her chest, she boarded the plane that would take her back to New York and away from Scott.

Chapter Fifteen

Linda's plane landed at La Guardia on time. As promised, Hilary was there to meet her. She quickly gathered Linda's luggage and ushered her to a waiting taxi.

Hilary eyed the roses Linda carried. "Did your friend Scott catch up with you before you left?" she asked, after they were on their way. "He called me and insisted that I give him your flight information. I hope it was okay."

"It was fine," Linda assured her. "He showed up at the airport with these roses."

"Nice," Hilary said with a sly smile. "I guess you two made the most of the last few weeks."

"We had fun," Linda said.

"I'd say it was a lot more than that."

"Why?"

"Because you look like you left your heart with him."

Hilary gave her a knowing smile. "Kind of like you looked when you broke up with loverboy Ralston, only sadder."

Hilary had seen Linda through many bad times both professionally and personally, so she felt like she was entitled to voice her opinions freely. Linda nodded in agreement.

"Rick Ralston couldn't shine Scott's shoes," Linda said firmly. Then she smiled, as she remembered that Scott didn't wear shoes too often.

"Good. News in the theater district travels fast, and Rick Ralston called me this afternoon. He wants the lead in your play. Will that be a problem for you?"

"Not at all," Linda replied, fingering the diamond around her neck. "Of course, he'll have to audition. He may not be right for it."

Hilary threw back her platinum blond head and laughed out loud. "I'd pay serious money to see Rick grovel. Luckily, as your agent, I can watch it for free. Auditions start tomorrow."

"Tomorrow," Linda repeated. She was hoping to have time to unpack and straighten up her apartment.

"I'll send a cleaning crew to spruce up your apartment," Hilary said, as if reading Linda's thoughts. "Did you sign the contract?"

"On the plane," Linda replied. She opened her purse and handed Hilary the contract. "It's almost too good to be true. How did you get them to agree to that much money?"

Hilary laughed again. "I told you on the phone, with Ken Hartman signed on, they know it's going to be a hit. That's why they're so anxious to get it going. By the way, Ken is very attractive and a nice guy to boot."

"Will he be at the auditions tomorrow?"

"Of course. After he talked to you today, he spent the entire afternoon and evening at his piano. He's already finished three of the songs. You'll hear them at the auditions tomorrow."

"This is all going so fast, I feel like I'm spinning."

"Maybe you're hungry. Did they feed you on the plane?"

"No, but I'm too excited to eat."

"Good. Now tell me about the movie script and your co-writer, not necessarily in that order."

For the rest of the ride, Linda talked about Scott, the beach house, the script, and Charlie and LaVerne. "I have a whole list of producers that said they wanted to read my work."

"Just give me the names," Hilary suggested. "I'll write

them each a nice note and invite them to your opening. That should impress the hell out of them."

Hilary helped Linda carry her luggage up to her second-floor apartment in the old brownstone building where Linda had lived for years. The Greenwich Village neighborhood was a little shabby but fairly safe, and it was a short commute to the theater district.

There was a light burning in the living room, and Hilary, who had a key in case of emergencies, had thoughtfully stocked the cabinets and refrigerator with food for Linda's homecoming.

"Solomon is sending a car for you tomorrow at ten," Hilary said, as she was preparing to leave. "I'll meet you at the theater."

"Thanks for everything, Hilary," Linda said, giving her agent and friend a warm hug.

"You're welcome." Hilary opened the door and stepped out into the hallway. "And as soon as the play opens, I'll help you find a better place to live," Hilary told her. "A bigger place in a nicer neighborhood."

Linda shut the door and turned the dead bolt, then went to the window and watched until Hilary came out of the building and got into the cab that was still waiting at the curb for her.

"A bigger house in a nicer neighborhood." Hilary's parting words reminded Linda of Scott's story about his father. Was Linda about to travel down the same kind of path, a path that would take her further and further away from Scott?

"No," Linda said aloud. "This apartment is fine. I think I'll stay right here." She walked across the bright throw rugs she had put down to cover the worn patches in the carpeting. She touched the old furnishings she had accumulated over the years.

Secondhand stores, yard sales, and donations from family and friends had filled her apartment with sofas, chairs, tables, lamps, and the big feather bed with the brass headboard that took up most of the tiny bedroom.

Linda carried her suitcases into the bedroom to unpack. Particles of sand still clung to some of the clothes she had hurriedly stuffed into her bags. It seemed she had carried remnants of the beach to her New York apartment. Linda's thoughts were once more claimed by memories of Scott and their days at the beach. She wished that she could talk to Scott, and considered calling LaVerne. She quickly dismissed the idea. Talking to LaVerne would just get both of them crying again. She would have to find a suitable gift to send to her and Charlie.

On the battered dresser next to Linda's closet were photographs of Linda's parents, both gone for several years now. *Funny,* she thought, *I don't have any pictures of the two of them together, not even a wedding picture.*

She did have a few precious snapshots of herself with her dad, taken at some holiday gathering when she was young. She picked one up and gazed into the handsome, smiling face of the father she had adored.

This Broadway production was for him. *The Magic Camera* was based on one of his stories. It would soon come to life on the Broadway stage and everyone would be able to experience its warmth and charm. She would work very hard to make sure they kept the story true and in focus. She owed it to her dad.

"There's a new man in my life," Linda said to her father's image in the photo. "He reminds me of you. Good, kind, loving, and funny. Help me to be fair to both of you."

Chapter Sixteen

The director hired by the Solomon Organization was George Carmichael, who had several Broadway hits to his credit. Linda had met him briefly at a social event, but this meeting was different. This man would control her life for the next several weeks and she was nervous. She wanted to make a good impression.

Her fears proved to be groundless as Carmichael turned out to be very open and friendly.

On the first morning, before auditions began, he sat Linda down and explained how he intended to stage the play. His vision of the production matched her own.

George was a big man in stature, with a head full of gray hair and a bushy mustache. Next to him, Linda looked like a midget, but George made her feel ten feet tall, and she soon realized he used the same charisma on everyone. No wonder he was able to coax brilliant performances out of everyone in his casts and crews.

Ken Hartman showed up with a briefcase full of sheet music, and the next task of the morning was to go over the songs he had written. Ken was tall and thin, with long fingers that moved across the piano keys with grace and ease. He sang the songs for George and Linda and they were enchanted with the melodies. Linda was floating on cloud nine. Then, the actors began to arrive, and Rick Ralston approached her.

"Does being in love with the playwright give me an inside track?" he asked, embracing her warmly.

"I'm going to defer to George's judgement for the casting," Linda told him in a cool voice.

Undaunted, Rick invited her to lunch. Linda politely refused. Every woman in the theater was watching them, envious of the attention she was receiving from the smooth actor, and Linda took great pleasure in walking away from Rick and taking a seat between George and Ken. For once in their relationship, Linda seemed to have the upper hand, and she was thoroughly enjoying it.

The auditions took the rest of the morning. They broke for lunch at 12:30. George, Ken, Linda, and Hilary retreated to a backstage office, where someone had thoughtfully ordered in food from the deli next door.

As they ate, they discussed the actors who had already auditioned. "I want to cast Ralston in the lead," George announced between bites of a towering roast beef sandwich. "He's got the right look and the talent."

"His singing voice isn't as good as some of the others," Ken observed.

"No, but his acting and stage presence are better. What do you think, Linda? Who did you have in mind when you wrote the part of Steven?"

"Rick Ralston," she admitted. "I was actually dating him at the time, and . . ." Linda shrugged and looked over at Hilary, who was unsuccessfully trying to stifle a laugh.

"Linda, you're just too honest," Hilary told her. "But I agree with George. Rick will be fabulous in the part."

George turned to the composer, who was frowning. "Listen, Ken, your songs are so good, anyone can sing them successfully. And I promise everyone else we cast will sing so well, it will make up for Ralston."

Hartman immediately brightened. "I was really impressed with the tall redhead. She had perfect pitch."

Rick Ralston was therefore cast in the lead part of Steven.

They auditioned until midnight on that first day and cast most of the parts. Linda returned home exhausted. She fell into bed and relived the day's events. She knew that Rick would assume that he got the part because Linda was still in love with him and wanted the opportunity to be with him every day. Linda drifted off into sleep, contemplating the consequences of being exposed to Rick's good looks and charm for the next six weeks of rehearsal.

An hour later, Linda was awakened by a persistent ringing. It was the telephone. Fumbling around in the dark, Linda located the phone on her bedside table and dragged it over to her ear. "Hello," she mumbled huskily.

"Hi, sunlight," Scott said brightly. "You sound sleepy. Did I wake you up?"

A delicious warmth spread over Linda at the sound of his voice. "It's after midnight," she told him, pushing herself into a sitting position. "I had an exhausting day of auditions for the play."

"Oh, sorry," Scott apologized. "I forgot about the time difference. It's only ten here. Do you want me to hang up so you can go back to sleep?"

Linda laughed softly. "No. I'm actually very happy to hear your voice. Did you get a telephone installed?"

Now it was Scott's turn to laugh. "No. I'm at the Cavanaugh's house. LaVerne is worried about you."

"Oh, I should have called her," Linda said. "It's just been so busy here."

"Already?"

"Yes, I'm afraid so."

LaVerne came on the line and they chatted for a few minutes. "I'm keeping your room here ready in case you get some time off and want to come home," LaVerne said. "And Charlie wants to know if there are any good-looking girls in your show. Not that it would help him any." Then LaVerne gave the phone back to Scott.

"I want to know if there are any good-looking men in your show," Scott said in a teasing voice.

"Yes," Linda replied hesitantly.

"What about your old flame, Rick Ralston?"

"I'm afraid so," she answered. "The director cast him in the lead role."

"How much do I need to worry?" Scott asked. His voice had lost its light tone.

"Why worry? Just get on the next plane to New York. I miss you."

"I think that's the nicest thing you've ever said to me," Scott told her. "But the movie definitely starts shooting next week. Frank says I have to be on the set in case they need script changes."

"I didn't really believe it would happen so fast."

"Remember the director's scheduling conflicts?" Scott replied. "The reason we had to rush the script?"

Linda remembered. It was the reason she had agreed to move out to the beach with Scott. The reason she was now torn between two coasts.

"I remember," she said softly.

"Hey, don't concern your pretty head about it. I'll make sure they do it right."

"I just wanted to be there when the movie was being filmed," Linda told him.

"I just wanted you to be here, period," Scott said, his voice filled with yearning.

"I have to be here for the play, Scott. It's very important to me, but so is the movie. It seems unfair that both things had to happen at the same time."

"You're right, honey, but that's the way it is."

"They plan on previewing the play in Connecticut in six weeks," Linda said. "I'll be at the theater night and day until then. Frank has the number there in case you need to talk to me."

"I need a lot more than talk from you," Scott said. "I'd be more specific, but Charlie is listening and I don't want to put the old goat into cardiac arrest."

"We'll be together again soon," Linda promised.

They talked for a few more minutes, not saying any of the things they really wanted to say, but intimating them with the emotion in their voices. When they hung up, Linda tried to go back to sleep, but her bed felt cold and empty. She wondered if Scott was really missing her as much as she missed him.

Chapter Seventeen

The next few weeks were more hectic than Linda could have imagined. The actors were rehearsing the songs as they were written and working with the choreographer, learning the basic dance moves she wanted.

Linda worked on the play script, incorporating the songs Ken provided. Everyone seemed pleased with the storyline and plot twists, so mainly Linda was adding the dialogue necessary to lead into each musical number.

Once the script and the music were done and melded together, the real work began. Endless production meetings about sets, costumes, lights, understudies, and a million other things claimed all of her time and attention.

It was arduous and, at the same time, exhilarating. In Linda's book, George Carmichael was the ultimate professional, handling the most difficult actors and problems with ease and wit. Ken Hartman was truly a musical genius, and the score for *The Magic Camera* was extraordinary.

"Hilary," Linda whispered one afternoon when her agent had stopped by to catch a rehearsal. "Is this show as good as I think it is?"

"Only if you think it's going to be this season's biggest hit," Hilary replied. "By the way, how are things going with Rick?"

"He's great in the show, and that's all I care about,"

Linda said firmly. "How are things going with you and Ken?"

Hilary shook her head. "Too slowly for my taste. The composer is a little shy and totally wrapped up in his work."

"Well, don't give up on him," Linda advised. "I think he's just a late bloomer. He'll be worth the wait."

"Maybe I'm getting too old to play these romantic games." Hilary had been married twice, divorced once, and widowed once. She had three teenage children and seemed to run their lives as efficiently as she ran her agency. "And how are things with you and the California surfer?"

"Desperate," Linda replied honestly. "He calls every day to update me on the movie, and it's making me miss him all the more. The good news is that the film is right on schedule and should be finished in a few days. I gave Scott my number in Connecticut so he could call me there. Are you coming there with us?"

"I'd love to, but I don't think I can do it. It's a shame, because it would be a good opportunity to corner the music man in a new romantic setting."

Linda covered her mouth to suppress her laughter. Then, Hilary had to leave, and Linda ran off to meet with the Solomon's publicity team to discuss the bio they were working on for the Connecticut programs.

Two days later, the entire company of *The Magic Camera* drove off to Connecticut. More rehearsals and more meetings, and not even the comfort of her own bed and apartment to return to at night.

They were all staying at a charming rural resort called Country Inn. The attractive setting seemed to make Rick think Linda would be more susceptible to his advances. She found herself constantly dodging his roving hands and finally threatened him with bodily harm if he didn't leave her alone.

"You're just uptight about the show," Rick replied, not bothered by her attitude. "You'll feel differently after the first live performance is over."

"You're amazing," Linda cried.

"Thank you, so are you."

Linda hurried away from him. It was a beautiful place, and under ordinary circumstances Linda would have been soothed by the peaceful greenness of it, but Rick was right about one thing. The first preview performance of *The Magic Camera* was about to take place and Linda was filled with pre-show jitters.

"We're ready," Rick told her at breakfast the morning the show was scheduled to open. "In fact, I don't think I've ever been involved with a show that was more on its feet."

"I hope you're right," Linda said.

George and Ken came back from the buffet line and joined them. Both had heaping plates of scrambled eggs, sausages, potatoes, and biscuits. Linda had opted for an English muffin and a cup of coffee. Rick, who had up been hours earlier than anyone else to take a jog in the country, nibbled on some fruit.

"Is that all you two are eating?" George asked in his booming voice.

"Linda's got a case of nerves, and I eat very little the day of a performance. Go on stage hungry and it gives you an extra edge."

Ken stared at Rick as if he had just arrived from Mars. "I never heard of that."

"From what I've observed with you and a certain female agent, you've never heard of a lot of things."

Linda would have kicked Rick under table, but she didn't want to risk injuring him before tonight's performance. Fortunately, one of the chorus girls, who made no secret of her passion for the leading man, came over and took him away with her.

"I don't think I like him," Ken said after Rick was out of earshot.

"He's good for the show," George said simply. "We don't have to like him."

Linda excused herself, went back to her room, and called Dancer Productions again. Julie answered.

"Hi, Julie. Linda Lucas. I just wondering how the movie was coming along?"

"They finished shooting the major scenes, just in time for the director to go on to his next project. The assistant director will finish up the minor stuff."

"Does that mean that Scott is free?"

"Don't know. Haven't seen him lately. Do you want to talk to Frank?"

"No, that's okay. I just wanted to check in. You have my number here in Connecticut."

"Yes. How's the play going?"

"The first performance before an audience is tonight. I'm a nervous wreck."

"I'm sure it will be great," Julie said.

"Will you tell Scott to call me here, if you see him?"

"Sure thing."

Linda hung up, did a fast repair job on her makeup, and walked back to the dining room. She drove over to the theater with George and they discussed some details for the show.

That morning drive turned out to be the last peaceful moments Linda had that day.

Everything that could go wrong with sets, sound, props, costumes, and lights happened during rehearsal. The theater where the preview was being held was an old converted barn, and the electrical system wasn't very good. A certain combination of lights and sound blew fuses. Somehow props and costumes got lost, and the musical conductor said the piano was out of tune.

Linda dashed around, helping wherever she could, feeling more out of control every second. She barely had time to return to the inn to shower and change before show time.

Alone in her room, Linda discovered she had forgotten to pack the shoes she wanted to wear with the new dress that she'd purchased just for tonight.

The only other shoes she had with her were sandals and tennis shoes. With no time to drive into town and buy shoes, Linda went out to the balcony and screamed into the wind.

That made her feel better. She quickly showered, dried her hair, and found another dress to wear. This one was a simple sundress with pretty embroidered flowers, and it looked okay with her white sandals. Linda didn't wear it much because it had spaghetti straps that were always slipping off her shoulders, but at this point she was too agitated to care.

Her first stop at the theater was backstage to wish the cast a good show. Rick took one look at her in the dress and let out a loud wolf whistle, which resulted in a lot of laughter and comments from a mostly male stage crew.

"I need a kiss for courage," Rick said, with a wink. Linda ignored his request, told him to break a leg, and swiftly made the rounds of the dressing rooms, wishing the other cast members well.

George, Linda, and Ken were to watch the show from the back of the theater. It would be the first time they would see it without being able to make comments and changes.

Linda was about to make her way out front when the stage manager approached her. "Miss Lucas, there's a guy causing a bit of a ruckus at the box office. Says he's a friend of yours from California. They called back here and asked if you'd come up and identify him."

There was only one person Linda could think of who would cause a ruckus. With her heart pounding, Linda hurried out to the lobby and looked around.

Scott was standing off to one side of the box office, his athletic body encased in a white summer suit. Under the jacket he wore a soft opened-necked shirt of pale blue. He had cut his hair short, which made his tan seem more bronze and his eyes more strikingly blue than Linda had remembered.

Linda called out his name and he opened his arms to greet her. He held her close for a long time, and she felt as if she were finally back where she belonged.

The box-office manager came out and cleared his throat

to get their attention. "Miss Lucas, I apologize for detaining your friend, but his name isn't on the list."

"He'll be sitting with me," Linda said. "You may have to reassign someone else."

"No problem," the manager said curtly, letting her know that he did indeed think it was a problem.

Linda ignored him and turned back to Scott. "How did you get here?"

"The usual way. We wound up shooting a day ahead of schedule, so I told Frank to get his travel agent to book me on the next flight. He was thrilled to get rid of me. Too much togetherness the last few weeks."

Linda laughed and hugged him again. "Today has been a nightmare, but now that you're here I know everything is going to be fine."

"Nice dress," Scott said suddenly.

"Thanks," Linda replied. "It was a big hit backstage."

"I can see why." Scott chuckled and put his arm around her shoulder. "You look nervous."

"I'm a wreck," Linda confessed. Then she brightened again. "Come on, I want to introduce you to some people."

They found Ken standing in the aisle near their seats. He looked as nervous as Linda felt. She introduced him to Scott and the men shook hands. "Where's George?" Linda asked Ken.

"Backstage making a last-minute check. Some of the actors told me they go outside and scream to expel their nervousness. Do you think it would work for me?"

"I did it earlier at the inn. It helps a little."

Ken never got the chance to try out the method, as one of the orchestra members suddenly appeared at his side and took him off to review a piece of music.

"Maybe we should sit down," Linda told Scott. "I'm feeling a little queasy."

"Lead the way," Scott agreed. Linda took his hand and guided him to the seats in the back row of the theater. Scott looked puzzled. "I thought the playwright would be seated front row center," he said.

"No, it's a tradition for the writers and directors to sit in the last row, especially during preview performances. That way, if the show is a flop, they can make a quick exit."

Scott laughed and squeezed her hand. "I'm sure that won't be necessary tonight. The show is going to be sensational."

A few minutes later, George joined them and was introduced to Scott. Then Ken returned from the orchestra pit and they all settled into their seats. The theater was full.

George produced small notepads and pens for himself, Ken, and Linda. Part of the preview process was to make a note of anything in the show that didn't seem to work so it could be polished for the next performance.

The lights began to dim, signaling the start of the show. George held up both hands and crossed his fingers. They had brought in a backup generator to guard against the electrical problems experienced earlier that day.

The orchestra began to play the overture music and the audience grew silent. Unlike many Broadway theaters in New York, this one had a curtain. It opened, the lights came up and stayed up, and the show began with a dazzling musical number. The audience seemed to love it, and applauded enthusiastically.

Now Linda held her breath, waiting for the first line that was supposed to result in laughter from the audience. It was delivered by the lovely redhead with perfect pitch. Laughter rang through the theater, and, all at once, Linda's spirit felt like a balloon filled with helium: light, airy, and reaching for the stars. As the show continued, the audience responded to everything just the way Linda had hoped they would.

At intermission, George held up his notepad to show Linda. Like her own, it was empty. They both looked at the composer; he had two notations on his pad, both concerning Rick Ralston's phrasing of a song.

"Let's get some air," Linda suggested to Scott. Both Ken and George were making their way backstage to prepare for the second act.

Outside, the night air was clear and warm. "This is one of the best shows I've ever seen," Scott said. "And the audience is loving every minute of it."

"Do you really think so?" Linda asked.

"I really think so," Scott assured her.

Linda wanted to dance for joy, but there were too many people milling around. She settled for hugging Scott. "I'm so happy you're here to share this with me."

"Only you could get me to stray this far from the Pacific Ocean."

"We have an ocean on this side of the country too," Linda told him.

"Do you think you'll have time to show me around tomorrow?" Scott asked.

"If the second act goes as well as the first act," Linda mused, "we'll have the entire day to ourselves. Once the play is on its feet, my job is finished, at least until we get back to New York."

"Do you want a report on the movie?" Scott asked.

Linda was immediately assailed by guilt. "Oh, Scott, I'm so sorry," she cried. "I've been so wrapped up in the play, I didn't even ask about the movie."

Scott took both of her hands in his and pulled her close to him. "Hey, honey, I didn't show up here to put you on a guilt trip. Although with you gone, Frank made me stay on the set so much my tan started to fade."

Linda caught the unmistakable gleam of mischief in his eyes. "Isn't that a shame," she said with mock sincerity. "And did they actually make you work?"

"I'll have you know, I had to rewrite two whole sentences in one scene. And the way I type, it was murder."

Linda laughed. "Oh, Scott, I really missed you. And I'm really sorry I couldn't be there with you when they were filming."

"And I'm really sorry you couldn't be with me when they weren't filming. That beach house has suddenly become very lonely."

"You're here with me now," she replied, kissing him lightly on the lips.

"Don't start that, lady," Scott warned. "Unless you want to miss the second act of your play."

Linda pulled back and gave him a radiant smile. "No, but I'll take a rain check for later."

Intermission was almost over, so Scott and Linda merged with the flow of people returning to the theater. As they walked, Linda could overhear comments about the show.

"Sometimes musicals don't have much of a story," one woman told her companion. "But this show has great music *and* a great story."

"Your dad would be very proud," Scott whispered.

Linda nodded, so emotional she was afraid to speak.

Then they overheard two younger women talking about Rick Ralston. "He's absolutely gorgeous. I wonder if he's single."

"A definite hunk," the other woman agreed. "He should be in the movies."

Linda glanced over at Scott, who made a face at their backs. She grinned and gave him a gentle push towards their seats.

Act two didn't go quite as smoothly as act one, but the difficulties were all technical and the audience didn't seem to notice.

The cast got a standing ovation. Then, as was the custom in Connecticut when they really liked a show, people started shouting, "Author! Composer! Author! Composer!"

Linda and Ken stood and graciously accepted the audience's cheers and applause. Scott stood and applauded and cheered like everyone else.

Linda hugged Ken. George hugged Linda. Ken hugged George. Then all three of them hugged each other at the same time.

"Let's go," George instructed. "We'll slip out the side door and get to the inn before the cast and crew. I want the champagne ready to toast them as soon as they arrive.

Linda, hang on to your fellow so he doesn't get lost in the crowd."

George hustled Scott and Linda into a waiting car and they sped back to the inn, where a light buffet supper was being prepared.

By the time the cast and crew members arrived, the champagne was uncorked and poured. Two executives from the Solomon Organization magically appeared and took charge of the toasts.

The celebration was loud and exuberant. Linda was soon dragged away from Scott's side to pose for pictures and meet local media people who had attended the preview. Everyone was hugging and kissing and assuring each other the show was going to take Broadway by storm.

As Linda tried to get back to Scott, Rick Ralston caught up with her. "You did it, Linda," he said warmly. "The show is going to be a smash."

"You were wonderful in it," Linda told him sincerely. "Thank you."

"No, thank you," Rick insisted, then before she knew what was happening, Rick swept her off her feet and kissed her. It was not a friendly, casual kiss, but the kind of romantic kiss they once shared on a regular basis.

Linda finally managed to pull free of him and found that Scott was standing right next to them. As Linda tried to think of a way to defuse the situation, Scott offered his hand to Rick.

"You must be Rick Ralston, the former boyfriend," Scott said pleasantly. "I'm Scott Richards, the current boyfriend."

Rick was stunned. He wasn't used to someone as brash and open as Scott, but he recovered enough to reply, "Linda and I have a long history together. She's very special to me."

"Scott is my co-writer on the screenplay," Linda said quickly. "He came all the way from California to see the preview tonight."

"Actually," Scott said in the same pleasant tone, "I came all the way from California to see Linda. The play was just a bonus. By the way, Rick, your performance was very good."

"Thank you, Scott."

"You're welcome. Keep up the good work."

Rick looked like someone had just thrown a drink in his face. Scott coolly took Linda's arm and escorted her across the crowded dining area to the double doors that led to the patio.

Only a few people were outside, and Scott pulled Linda into the shadow of a maple tree. Cupping her face in his hands, Scott kissed her. It was a slow, lingering kiss filled with so much longing that Linda's knees grew weak. She leaned into Scott for support and then he suddenly released her.

"Okay, the choice is yours," he said. "Me or Ralston?"

Linda burst out laughing and threw her arms around his neck. "No contest," she whispered.

Chapter Eighteen

The next week was like a wonderful dream for Linda. Ken had to go back to New York, so Scott took over the composer's room.

The remaining preview performances were standing-room-only, as Connecticut's wealthy summer visitors flocked to the theater for an advance look at what everyone was saying would be Broadway's next hit show.

As she had told Scott, George and the technical people were now in charge of the show, and that meant Linda's days were partially free. She and Scott traveled through the beautiful countryside.

They drove, they walked, and sometimes they rode rented bikes up and down the hills and tree-lined roads. There were trips to the ocean and picnics on the beach, and they scoured quaint antique shops, looking at everything and buying nothing.

They decided to postpone any serious discussions about their future until after Linda's play opened on Broadway. Both of them were smart enough to realize that Linda's emotions were vulnerable and her state of mind fragile. Despite the good reviews the show had received in the out-of-town tryouts, she was still nervous.

"Broadway is a whole different ball game," she told

Scott over and over. "If the New York critics don't like the show, it could close in a week."

"They're going to love it, Linda," Scott assured her.

"I hope so."

"We're not going to jeopardize the trust we've built in each other by complicating our relationship any more than it already is," Scott told her, as they said good-night outside her door. "I'm willing to wait, because when you're ready to commit completely, I know it will be forever."

"I just can't think rationally about anything but the show right now," Linda admitted. "But I do know that having you with me has kept me from worrying myself into a frenzy."

Finally, it was time to pack up the cast, crew, sets, and equipment and go back to New York to prepare for the Broadway opening.

Linda had convinced Scott to travel to New York with her and stay on at least until after the show opened on Broadway.

"I need you, Scott," Linda told him. "You keep me grounded and sane."

Frank and Carla Dancer owned a condo in an expensive area near Central Park. Scott could stay there as long as he wanted.

On their first night in New York, Scott and Linda had dinner with Hilary and Ken Hartman. The romance between her agent and the composer seemed to be progressing nicely. However, they spent most of the evening discussing the show and which critics they could count on to give it a good review.

On the cab ride to Scott's temporary abode, he expressed the second thoughts he was having about staying in New York.

"I don't know how you people can let your lives and your future depend on a few lousy critics. They're just newspaper reporters, and their opinions shouldn't mean that much to you."

"You're right," Linda said. "But that's the way it is here."

"Come home with me and write movie scripts. They open in thousands of theaters at once. All that counts is the hype the film gets ahead of time. A good opening weekend and the film makes money, even if the critics hate it. Here you open at one theater, and if some guy from the *Times* has a headache and doesn't like the show, you close it down."

"It's very risky," Linda admitted. "That's why theaters do so many revivals."

"I think it's nuts."

"Well, it's too late to back out now. Besides, only in live theater can a playwright or an actor experience the wonderful chemistry that can develop between them and the audience. You get an instant response to your work. It's risky, but when it works, it's magical."

"I hope that's how it works out for you, honey, but I'm not sure I can cut it in New York," Scott told her. "You'll be busy at the theater every day, and I'll be like a fish out of water."

"Scott," Linda chided. "New York is an exciting city. There's a million things to do there."

"Which will be no fun without you," Scott grumbled.

"Okay then," Linda said, having already given this a great deal of thought. "While I'm at the theater, you can stay home and write."

"Write what?"

"Whatever you want."

"You're getting me confused with someone else," he said stubbornly. "I don't have a head full of stories I want to get down on paper. I rewrite other people's scripts—very mechanical, not very creative."

"That's not true," Linda insisted. "You are one of the most talented, creative people I've ever met. You're just lazy." Linda put a hand over her mouth. She hadn't meant for that last sentence to slip out. "I'm sorry, I didn't mean to say that."

"Yes, you did," Scott told her, without a trace of anger. "And I can't argue with you. I am lazy. I told you the first day we met, I'm a bum, and I like being a bum."

"And you think I'm trying to change you."

"Aren't you?"

"Yes, I guess I am," Linda admitted. "But only because I want you to stay in New York with me."

Linda felt close to tears, and Scott put his arm around her shoulders.

"Okay, honey. You win. I'll stay in New York for awhile, at least until after your show opens. But at some point, I'm going to ask you to go back and live at the beach with me. You'd better start thinking about what your answer will be."

Linda pulled back and looked into his eyes. This time there was no hint of humor or jest. In her heart she knew that trying to keep Scott in New York would be like trying to keep a bird from flight. The only sure way to do it was to clip his wings, and Scott would never stand for that.

Chapter Nineteen

The weeks before the Broadway opening were like riding on an out-of-control Ferris wheel: spinning, swaying, screaming moments that left Linda dizzy and off-balance.

The publicity team had kicked into high gear and booked Linda and Ken on a number of talk shows. They also did radio shows and were interviewed by all the local newspapers.

Linda kept remembering what Scott said about media hype and how it ensured that a film made money. Opening night had been sold out for weeks, but it was the days and weeks that followed a show's opening that really counted. The theater-going public tended to hold back and see if a show was going to be proclaimed a hit by the critics before they plunked down their cash for a ticket. So Linda often thought the whirlwind publicity campaign was a waste of time.

In between publicity gigs, Linda tried to spend time with Scott. One night, after a particularly tiring day, she stopped by the condo with pizza.

Scott opened the door dressed in shorts and a T-shirt. It was the first time Linda had seen him dressed like that since she left the beach.

"You look relaxed," she commented.

"I didn't expect to see you tonight. You look exhausted,"

Scott replied, taking the pizza and carrying it into the kitchen area.

Linda crossed the living room after Scott and passed by Frank Dancer's office. The computer was on, and the screen contained what looked like a script page. She went into the room to have a look.

When Scott realized she was no longer behind him, he dropped the pizza on the ceramic tile counter and went looking for her.

"What is this?" Linda asked, as Scott appeared in the doorway to the office.

"Nothing much." Scott shrugged.

"It looks like a play script to me."

"Thank you. I was wondering what to call it."

Linda put her finger on the page-down button and kept reading. Scott walked over and stood behind her. "Come on, honey. The pizza is going to get cold."

"Can I print out a copy of it? I want to read the whole thing."

"No way," Scott said, spinning the desk chair around so Linda was facing him. "Maybe when it's finished."

"When will that be?" Linda persisted.

"Maybe tomorrow, maybe never. Come on. I hate cold pizza."

"You love cold pizza."

"Not tonight. Come on." Scott pulled her to her feet and kissed her. While he held onto her with one arm, he reached behind her with the other, closed the file, and shut down the computer.

"That's cheating," Linda told him, leaning against him and taking comfort from the strength of his body and arms.

"You're tense. Have a hard day?" he asked as he began to massage her neck and shoulders.

"Yes."

"I saw you on that morning talk show. You looked gorgeous, but Ken looked like he just ate a sour pickle."

"He had a headache. I think Hilary kept him out too late last night."

Scott laughed. "Hilary is a barn burner. Poor guy will be lucky to get out of the relationship alive."

Linda didn't reply. Was that the way Scott viewed her and their relationship? She was tired and hungry and decided the question was best left unasked. "Let's go attack that pizza," she suggested.

The next morning, Linda called Scott from the theater. She got a busy signal. She tried again a few minutes later and got the same thing. After several attempts, Linda called the operator and asked her to check the line.

"The phone is off the hook," the operator reported.

George came into the small office where Linda was hiding out. "Something wrong?" he asked, noticing the perplexed look on her face.

"I don't know. I was trying to call Scott, but his phone is off the hook. I thought maybe we could have lunch together today."

"Nancy wants your opinion on some new moves she wants to add to the last musical number," George said.

Nancy was the choreographer for the show. She was young and enthusiastic and kept making changes in the dance routines.

"What do you think of them?" Linda asked. George had vetoed Nancy's last few ideas.

"I think it's better than what we had, but I'd like your opinion before I okay the change."

Linda nodded and pushed herself away from the desk. The dancers were on stage ready to do the new routine for Linda. She watched it from a seat in the middle of the theater. George was on one side of her, Ken on the other.

"I like it," Linda whispered.

"So do I," Ken said.

"Nancy," George called.

Nancy was a tall, willowy blond, more plain than pretty. She hurried down the aisle toward them with a look of concern on her face.

"Okay," George said, standing to greet her. "It's in, but

this is the last change. I don't want the cast worn out trying to learn new routines. Understood?"

Nancy smiled and nodded. "Understood. Thanks." She turned and ran back down the aisle.

"How about some lunch?" Ken asked. "I'm starving."

"I'll have someone order it in," George told him. "I've got some other things to discuss with you and Linda. I'll meet you in the office in a few minutes."

Linda sighed. She had been thinking she would have time to run over to the condo and check on Scott. She would have to try and call him again instead. What was it with him and telephones anyway? He'd probably taken it off the hook on purpose, so he wouldn't have to answer it.

Ken and Linda made their way back to the office to wait for George and lunch to arrive.

"How are things with you and Hilary?" Linda asked.

Ken looked at her curiously. "Fine. Why?"

"Scott said something last night about you and Hilary being opposites."

"I guess we are," Ken said thoughtfully. "She's certainly not like anyone else I've ever dated." He laughed. "Dated. We may both be a little too old and jaded for that expression."

Like Hilary, Ken had been married before. He also had teenage kids, twin boys.

"You're not too old," Linda chided. "Neither of you."

"I feel old. Trying to keep a relationship intact and work in the demanding world of live theater isn't easy. Of course, you already know that."

"I know that Scott isn't very happy in New York," Linda admitted.

"Has Scott ever had a play produced?"

"No, but he's working on one now."

"Right. And when it gets produced, he'll either get hooked on live theater like the rest of us, or hate it and head back to California."

"When it gets produced?" Linda smiled. "I'm not even sure if he'll finish it."

"It's finished."

Linda stared at Ken. "How do you know?"

"He told me about it when we went to dinner the other night, while you and Hilary were in the powder room."

Linda felt a stab of indignation. Scott hadn't even told her he was working on a stage play. She had discovered it accidently. Ken didn't seem to notice her annoyance. He was too busy worrying about himself and Hilary.

"Well, after this show opens," he said, "Hil and I are taking all our kids away for a long weekend. If we survive that, we can move onto the next phase of our relationship."

Linda nodded. It seemed that she and Scott had been stuck in phase one of their relationship for quite some time now. She fingered the pendant she always wore around her neck. Sunlight and starlight never really crossed paths.

"You know, Linda," Ken said, interrupting her thoughts. "The very fact that Scott has written a stage play is a sign of his commitment to you. I think he wants to find out why the theater means so much to you. He wants to find out first-hand so he can share it with you."

"Then why hasn't he talked to me about the play he's writing?"

"Maybe he wanted to surprise you with the finished product."

"Maybe."

"Maybe you could use some of your connections to help him get it produced," Ken suggested.

"Well, if he ever tells me about it, maybe I will," Linda said.

George pushed open the door to the office, and his assistant, a wiry young man named Ned, hurried in bearing a box from the deli across the street. The aroma of corned beef and pastrami filled the room.

While George and Ken settled down with their lunch, Linda punched in Scott's phone number again. The buzz of the busy signal sounded in her ear. She hung up the phone and selected a sandwich.

Ken's suggestion stayed in her mind all through the af-

ternoon meeting. She could help Scott get his play produced. She could call any number of producers she knew
or, better yet, have Hilary call one and arrange a production
for Scott's play. If necessary, Linda would finance it.

Since they arrived in New York, Linda had felt Scott
slipping away from her. She had been too busy, too involved with the show, but the show opened tomorrow
night. After that, she would have time to devote to Scott.

Chapter Twenty

Linda awoke the next morning in a panic. *The Magic Camera* opened on Broadway at the Solomon Theater tonight. Even after all the weeks of preparation, it didn't seem real.

She squinted at the clock on her dresser: 8:30. In twelve hours, the lights would be coming up on the stage and the orchestra would be playing the overture.

The meeting yesterday afternoon had lasted into the night. Linda had finally reached Scott around 6:00 P.M. only to have to report that she was tied up at the theater and couldn't have dinner with him.

Scott admitted that he had taken the phone off the hook, and apologized for worrying her. "I'll make it up to you with breakfast tomorrow. Then you can help me pick out my monkey suit for the opening."

"You don't have your tux with you?"

"I had planned on going home and coming back again," Scott said cheerfully. "But this amazing dark-haired girl I know wouldn't let me leave her."

Linda laughed, breaking some the tension she had been feeling. "Why don't you call Frank or Carla or LaVerne and have one of them bring it to you?"

"Now I'm going to be in trouble," he said softly.

"What did you do with your tux, Scott?"

"Rolled it up and threw it somewhere. Darned if I can remember where. Even if they found it for me, it would have to be cleaned and pressed. But don't worry, Frank has an account at one of the rental places. He called and made arrangements to rent one there for himself for tonight. I told him I'd pick it up and have it at the condo for him. I'll just rent a second one for myself and charge it to Frank. He won't mind."

"Okay. I'll see you in the morning. Not too early. I want to sleep in."

"I must really love you," Scott said. "You're the only girl in the world who could get me to wear a tuxedo not once, but twice in the same year."

Replaying the conversation in her head now made Linda smile and eased some of the pre-show jitters she was feeling. Scott was sounding like his old self again, like the impetuous beach bum she knew and loved.

Linda jumped out of bed and headed for the shower. Later today she was having her hair done, and then she would shower again and get dressed for the theater.

It was a week after Labor Day, so the white dress she had worn for the movie premiere had to be replaced by something else. She hadn't had much time to shop, but Hilary had saved the day by having her dressmaker bring designer fashions to the theater for Linda to look through.

She had settled on a calf-length dress with a slightly scooped neckline and half sleeves. The dress had a tight-fitting waist that flared into a full skirt and was made of some kind of silky material that rustled when Linda walked. It was plain yet striking, in a beautiful shade of burgundy, as rich and mellow as a fine wine.

It was hanging in Linda's closet, encased in a plastic bag, perfectly fitted and pressed for tonight's opening.

Scott banged on her door at 9:00. He had a taxi waiting out front for them. They exchanged a light kiss and then took off to get breakfast and a tuxedo for Scott.

Over breakfast, Linda told Scott about her conversation

with Ken the day before. "Ken said you finished your play script. You didn't even tell me that you were writing one."

"I didn't tell you because I didn't want you to be disappointed when I didn't finish it."

"But you did finish it," Linda insisted.

"Are you trying to pick a fight with me?" Scott asked. His eyes crinkled as he gave her one of his disarming smiles.

"No," Linda said defensively. "I just want to know why you didn't tell me after you finished it."

"It's only finished because you've been neglecting me. I didn't know what else to do with myself."

"Now who's trying to pick a fight?" Linda asked.

Scott laughed and grabbed her hand across the table. "Your eyes are flashing. It reminds me of the first day we met. You got so mad at me, you took off down the beach even though you didn't have a clue what or who was out there. No bigger turn-on than having a pretty girl run out on you. I think that's when I fell in love with you."

Their breakfast arrived and Scott let go of her hand. Linda stared at the plate of scrambled eggs, hash brown potatoes, and toast the waitress placed in front of her.

"Did I really order all this food? I'm not even hungry."

Scott laughed again. "You are a basket case this morning, sweetie. I thought you might be. That's why I didn't bring your copy of the play with me."

"What play?" Linda asked, as she scooped up some eggs and stuffed them into her mouth.

"I made you a copy of my play. You are the only person I would trust to read it and give me an honest opinion. The phone was off the hook yesterday because I was polishing it for the first reader, you."

"Oh, Scott. That's so nice. Of course I want to read it. I can't wait to read it."

"Well, I'm not giving it to you today, or tomorrow either, for that matter. Today you're a nut; tomorrow you'll be busy basking in the glow of success."

"Or crying my eyes out."

"Not even a remote possibility," Scott said firmly. "Now eat your breakfast like a good girl so we can go to the tuxedo store."

Now mingled with Linda's anxiety over her Broadway debut was excitement over the fact that Scott had finished a play. She saw it as a sign that their relationship was moving towards the solid ground of shared interest. Based on her firsthand knowledge of Scott's talent, Linda was already mentally jumping ahead, thinking of producers who would be willing to produce it.

"Earth to Linda," Scott said. "Are you okay?"

Linda forced thoughts about Scott and his play out of her mind and smiled at him. "I'm sorry," she said. "I'm afraid I'm going to be like this all day. Can you stand it?"

"Actually, I'm rather enjoying it. Makes me feel needed."

"I have neglected you, haven't I?"

"Yes."

"I'm sorry."

"It's okay. I understand how much this means to you."

"It'll all be settled one way or the other in . . ." Linda looked at her wrist, but her watch wasn't there. She had forgotten to put it on. "What time is it?"

Scott shrugged and looked around for a clock. He never wore a watch. "The clock by the counter says nine-thirty," he told her.

"Eleven hours . . . it will all be over in eleven hours. No. It will take longer than that. The papers don't come out until one or two in the morning."

Scott sat back in his chair and shook his head. "But by then you'll be at the party talking to all your friends. Frank and Carla will be there. LaVerne and Charlie will be there."

"LaVerne is going with me to the hairdresser's this afternoon. I have to pick her up at the hotel," Linda said suddenly. "I just remembered. Oh wow! What if I forget to pick her up?"

"Honey, I'll stay at your side all day. I'll even take you and LaVerne to the hairdresser's . . . Whoa, what am I saying? I'll tell Carla to take you. She'll probably want to go too."

Scott and Linda looked at each other across the small table and both burst out laughing. "See, now you've got me nuts," Scott said.

"And nuts like us don't grow on trees, you know?" Linda added.

They finished breakfast. They picked up Frank's tuxedo and got a second one for Scott. Scott hadn't thought to bring black shoes, so he rented a pair of them as well.

They dropped the tuxes off at Frank's condo and drove to Kennedy airport to meet the group that was arriving from California.

Frank didn't like commercial flights. Dancer Productions had a jet and a pilot that were always at his disposal. Today the plane was carrying LaVerne and Charlie as additional passengers.

Linda was anxious to see LaVerne and Charlie. It seemed like an eternity since she left them at the beach. Linda's schedule was so hectic, they had only managed to talk on the phone a few times.

"This is the way to travel," Charlie said, as he walked off the plane. "I'm going to buy a plane and fly it myself."

"And you'd end up like Amelia Earhart," LaVerne told him. "Lost forever."

"Maybe she's not lost," Charlie said. "She could be living it up in Bali for all you know."

"Shut up, you old coot, and give Linda a hug."

There were hugs all around for Linda and Scott. The warmth of their greetings and the fact that they had all traveled across the country to support her made Linda cry.

"What's wrong, honey?" LaVerne asked.

"Don't mind her," Scott said. "She's been like this all day. Give her a second, and she'll be laughing again."

Scott and Frank took Charlie to the hotel and then went to the condo to relax. Linda, Carla, and LaVerne went to the beauty salon. Hilary was already there, sitting under a hair dryer.

Linda introduced everyone and then collapsed in the hair-dresser's chair. All four women had the works: facials, manicures, and fancy hairdos.

Carla called a limousine service to take them all back to their respective places. They dropped Linda off at her apartment first. It was almost 5:00 P.M., a little over three hours remained until the curtain rose on *The Magic Camera*.

"Are you going to be all right in there alone?" LaVerne asked.

"I'm fine," Linda said in a calm voice. And strangely enough, she did feel calm and in control for the first time that day.

"Scott will be back with the car at seven. He'll take you to the theater and then send the car around to pick up the rest of us," Carla said. "If you need anything in the meantime, call me."

"Or me," LaVerne added.

"I'm fine," Linda repeated again. "I'll see you at the theater."

The limo driver held the door open for Linda and she stepped out of the car. She stood on the walkway in front of her building and waved as the car drove away. LaVerne and Carla waved back.

Linda turned and climbed the stairs to her apartment. Maybe it was the fancy hairdo, or maybe it was the softness of her cheeks after the facial, or maybe it was the bright color on her nails that had been chosen to match her dress that made Linda feel cool and confident. She didn't know what it was, but she wrapped the feeling around herself like an expensive cloak while she showered and dressed for the biggest evening of her life.

Her father's enchanting story was coming to life on the stage. That in itself was a major accomplishment, and even if the show closed tomorrow, she would still have tonight. Tonight, Linda Lucas's name was on the marquee at the Solomon Theater. Tonight, Scott would be by her side, loving her and supporting her. And maybe that was the most important accomplishment of all.

Chapter Twenty-one

Linda was afraid that once she got to the theater her jitters would return, but they stayed buried under her calm exterior.

George Carmichael was also pretty cool. "There's nothing we can do now but sit back and enjoy the show," George told Linda, after she had introduced him to her friends.

Ken and Hilary arrived arm in arm. They were in high spirits. "This is so exciting," Hilary whispered. "I've had other clients go to Broadway, but I was never in love with the composer before."

Linda laughed and hugged Scott's arm. His newly rented tuxedo fit him perfectly, and he looked as much like a leading man as Rick Ralston.

The lights flashed and everyone took their seats. The orchestra began the overture and the lights in the theater dimmed as the lights on the stage came up. Linda held tight to Scott's hand, waiting for the opening number and then the first lines of her play to be spoken on a Broadway stage.

The Broadway opening of *The Magic Camera* went off without the slightest hitch. The audience laughed and applauded in all the right places, and at the end of the show gave the cast a standing ovation. Linda and Ken were hustled to the stage to take a bow with the cast. The spotlight was as bright and hot as the sun on Scott's beach and Linda felt as strong and sure as the ocean that surrounded it.

The opening-night party was held at the hotel where LaVerne and Charlie were staying. A fountain of bubbling champagne occupied the center of the room.

Linda, Ken, and George stood in a reception line with the primary cast members for over an hour accepting congratulations from everyone who came through the door.

The Solomon Organization was large and prestigious, and all of Broadway's elite and powerful were there. Linda was glad that Frank and Carla and LaVerne and Charlie were there to sit with Scott while Linda stood in the reception line and was then dragged around to pose for endless photos.

Finally, everyone got fed, and a small orchestra began to play. Linda was looking around for Scott when Rick Ralston came up and put his arms around her.

"I just want to thank you for writing such a fabulous play and letting me be a part of this production," Rick said, with what seemed to be sincerity.

"You earned the part, Rick," Linda replied. "And you did an excellent job."

"Your dad would have been very proud."

"Yes." Linda nodded.

"Look, Linda, I know we've had some rocky times, but I still care about you. If you ever need anything, anything at all . . ."

"She'll call me," Scott said.

Linda spun around and saw the dazzling smile Scott was bestowing on Rick.

"Rick, you know Scott," Linda said.

"Yes, of course. It seems he pops up every time you and I are having a serious conversation."

"Congratulations on your performance tonight," Scott said smoothly. "People are saying you'll win a Tony."

"Really?" Rick's ego caused him to puff out his chest, obviously delighted by Scott's compliment.

Linda wondered if Scott were telling the truth or just

taunting Rick. Tony Awards were the most prestigious and coveted prize in live theater, much like the Oscars to films.

"Excuse us," Scott said. "They want to take Linda's photo with Frank Dancer, the movie tycoon. He's my brother-in-law, you know."

"No, I didn't know that. You'll have to introduce me to him."

"Sure," Scott said easily. "Maybe we can have lunch this week."

Linda suppressed a grin. Scott thought the "Let's have lunch" line was the phoniest line in Hollywood. He was definitely taunting Rick Ralston.

"I think you're jealous," Linda whispered, as Scott whisked her away.

"I think you're right," Scott said. "I'm not usually so nasty."

"Believe it or not, that's the first time I've spoken to him in weeks. He's been hot and heavy with his leading lady."

Linda spent the rest of the night with Scott and the group from California. LaVerne and Charlie were in rare form and were entertaining everyone with stories of their show business exploits.

"Tell me the truth, LaVerne," Carla asked. "Did you really date Bob Hope?"

"I said hello to him once," she replied with a straight face.

"LaVerne," Linda cried. "You made up that whole story about going to see Delores sing and Bob falling in love with her instead of you."

"Of course she did," Charlie said. "If Bob Hope were ever lucky enough to date my LaVerne, he would never even look at another woman. She's the best."

LaVerne smiled at her husband of forty-some years. "Okay, Charlie. You can have another piece of cake. Bring me one too."

Everyone laughed as Charlie jumped up and hurried over to the buffet table, where the remnants of a chocolate whipped cream cake were being passed out.

As the hour got later, some of the guests began to leave. However, everyone in the show or even remotely connected with it stayed on to wait for the reviews.

At 2.00 A.M. George and Ken went outside to wait for the papers. One of the reasons this particular hotel was chosen for the party was because there was a newsstand in the lobby that stayed open twenty-four hours and received the morning editions of the papers before anyone else.

Linda's jitters had returned. "I'm going outside to wait with Ken and George," Linda announced, getting to her feet.

"Do you want me to come along?" Scott asked.

"Let's all go," Frank Dancer suggested.

So Frank, Carla, LaVerne, Charlie, Scott, and Linda all went outside and stood with George and Ken and the guy from the newsstand who was waiting for the delivery truck.

"Let's sing," LaVerne said. "Row, row, row your boat . . ."

Everyone sang, and it helped pass the time and soothe their nerves. They stopped singing when the newspaper truck came squealing around the corner.

Linda closed her eyes and clung to Scott while George and Frank Dancer shoved money at the newsstand guy so they could grab some papers.

"Start rehearsing your acceptance speech, Linda," George shouted. "The *Times* says *The Magic Camera* is the best show Broadway has produced in two years!"

Linda let out a breath that came out as a scream. Then everyone was screaming and dancing and hugging and kissing and crying.

The scene was repeated inside the hotel when the reviews were read to the cast and crew still gathered there.

All the critics liked the show and had given it a favorable review, and that ensured a long run and steady paychecks for everyone involved with the show for a long time to come. On that happy note, the party broke up.

Linda was elated, but exhausted. They said goodnight to LaVerne and Charlie, who only had to take an elevator up five floors to their room.

Linda climbed into the limousine with the Dancers and Scott for the ride back to her apartment. She snuggled comfortably against Scott's broad shoulder. Frank and Carla were filled with ideas and plans to promote *The Last Laugh.*

The success of *The Magic Camera* would generate lots of buzz for the movie.

"I'm so sorry," Linda told Frank. "I've been so preoccupied with the play, I haven't even asked about the movie. When will it be released?"

"Not for a few months. It's in the editing process right now, and then there's a lot of post-production items to take care of."

"Can I do something to help?"

"You just relax and enjoy your success. We'll be in touch when we need you."

Linda nodded and closed her eyes. It was all too much to comprehend at the moment. Scott kissed the top of her head.

"I'm going to stay on in New York for a while longer," he announced to his sister and brother-in-law. "Any problem with me using the condo?"

"Not at all," Frank answered. "Glad to have someone using it."

"You deserve time off after working so hard while the movie was being filmed," Carla said. "Linda, my brother showed more ambition on this film project than he's ever shown before. I'm very proud of him . . . and you too, of course."

"I guess I kind of left him in the lurch," Linda replied. "Thank you again, Scott."

"Okay," Scott said. "Stop with the flattery. I love that film project, and I love my co-writer. So this is one instance when I didn't mind the work, but don't think I'm a changed man. I'm still a bum at heart."

"We know that, Scott," Carla said sweetly. "But we all love you anyway."

When they arrived at Linda's apartment, Scott walked Linda up to her door. He kissed her gently.

"I wish I could stay here with you, instead going to the condo with Frank and Carla. They're going to make me sleep on the couch in the den."

"And I'd make you sleep on the couch here," Linda said.

"At least you'd be close by," he said, touching her face gently. "Now that your play is a roaring success, we have to take our relationship out of limbo and make some definite plans."

"Tomorrow, Scott," Linda said with a big sleepy yawn. "We'll talk tomorrow. And bring me that play to read."

Scott nodded. One last kiss, and Linda went into her apartment and closed the door. She could hear Scott's footsteps as he bounded down the stairs.

Linda threw her clothes off, washed the makeup from her face, and fell into bed. It had been an incredible night, more wonderful than she'd ever imagined. The success of *The Magic Camera* would generate interest in all of her other plays.

Linda had finally achieved the goal she had set for herself. The years of struggling and working crazy jobs to support herself and follow her dreams had finally paid off.

The problem was that she couldn't turn her back on this good fortune and return to the beach with Scott. To capitalize on her current success, she had to stay in New York to pursue the opportunities and work on other productions.

Falling in love with Scott Richards had not been part of her plan, but nonetheless, she was in love with him. She longed to commit herself to him body and soul, marry him, have his children.

When they were in California, Scott had said he wanted to keep Linda with him at the beach. At the time, Linda had considered doing just that, but now everything was different. Fate had stepped in and pushed her into the limelight, and she couldn't give it up to share Scott's unstructured existence at the beach. If Linda was to have Scott in her life, somehow, some way, she had to keep him in New York. Tomorrow she would start working on this new goal. Once it was achieved, her happiness and her life would be complete.

Chapter Twenty-two

Tears clouded Linda's eyes as she read the last words on the page. She closed the cover of Scott's play script and placed her hand across it. It was a marvelous play, a perfect blend of tears and laughter.

Scott had given her the play that morning, and then made an excuse about having to help Carla do some shopping before she headed back to California.

Linda suspected that Scott just didn't want to hang around while she read his play. He was coming back in a few minutes to pick her up. The Dancers, the Cavanaughs, and Scott and Linda were all having lunch at Rockefeller Center before the Californians headed back to their home base.

Linda's phone had been ringing nonstop all morning, and several congratulatory floral arrangements had been delivered to her door. Linda had finally turned off the ringer and let her answering service pick up the calls so she could concentrate on Scott's play.

The doorbell rang and Linda opened the door to find Scott standing there in a brand-new outfit. He struck a pose.

"A pre-Christmas gift from my big sister. What do you think?"

The dark blue slacks were perfectly creased, and the knit

shirt of pale blue was a perfect contrast. With Scott's blond
hair and blue eyes, the effect was mesmerizing.

"You look grand." Linda laughed and threw her arms
around his neck. "Umm, you smell great too," she said,
cuddling closer to him.

"Something very expensive, guaranteed to make the girls
fall at my feet. Another extravagance lavished on me by
Carla."

"I don't think I like that remark about the girls falling at
your feet. Do I have reason to worry?" she asked, repeating
the question he had used on her last night when asking
about Rick Ralston.

"You're my one and only," Scott replied. "Are you ready
to go? Frank is already at Rockefeller Center using his influence to get us a table."

"What about the rest of the group?"

"They're all with him. We have the limo to ourselves.
We can make out all the way there."

"I'm going to miss that limo," Linda said lightly.

"Me too."

Linda was dressed in a pair of brown slacks and a silk
peach-colored blouse with long sleeves and an open collar.

She grabbed her purse, locked the door, and headed
down the staircase ahead of Scott.

"I like that outfit, very classy." Scott said, appraising her
from behind.

"I bought it before I came to Hollywood, but since I
spent so much time at the beach, I never got to wear it."

"Is that a dig?"

"Definitely."

The driver held the door of the limo open and Linda and
Scott climbed inside. Soon they were speeding away from
Linda's neighborhood, heading for Rockefeller Center.

Linda waited for Scott to ask her about the play, but he
just took her hand and started humming some tune that
existed only in his own mind.

"I think it is absolutely brilliant," Linda said, unable to
contain herself any longer.

"My new look? Or the aftershave?" Scott asked.

"Scott," Linda cried. "Don't be obtuse. You know I'm talking about your play."

"Then you had time to read it," he said calmly.

"It made me laugh. It made me cry. And it proves what I have been saying all along. You're a very talented writer."

"Good. I'm glad you liked it. What kind of food do they have at this restaurant? Carla walked my legs off. I need nourishment."

Linda wasn't about to give up. "I want to show it to Hilary and some of the producers I know."

Scott turned and looked at her. "Why?"

"Something this good has to be staged."

"I don't think so."

"Why not?"

Scott smiled at her. "I know what you're doing, Linda. You're trying to make me work. Mold me into the man you think I should be. Give it up. You said you could accept me the way I am, and I'm holding you to that." His tone was light and teasing. Scott often made serious statements in that way, a manner that was designed to avoid an argument.

Linda turned her head and looked out the window on the other side of the car. Soon they would be passing through the theater district, the place that had captured her heart and soul so many years ago.

"I love you, Scott," she said softly. "But I love New York and the world of theater too. My success is still so new. I'm afraid that if I don't stay here and nurture it, it will crash and burn."

Scott didn't move or speak for several minutes. Linda continued to stare out the window, fighting back the tears her honesty had pushed to the surface. She was instantly sorry the moment the statement had passed her lips. This was supposed to be a happy day, a lunch to celebrate friendship and success. Ultimatums had no place in a day like this.

She felt the warmth of Scott's hand as he touched her

cheek. She turned to face him again and he held her face in his hands and kissed her deeply.

"Okay," he said, keeping her face cradled in his hands. "Show the play to Hilary and anyone else you want. I'll go along for now. Just don't expect too much. I tend to disappoint people who expect too much from me."

"That's because you underestimate . . ."

Scott kissed her again to cut off her argument. "Discussion closed," he whispered, pulling her close and resting his head on top of hers.

Lunch at Rockefeller Center was delightful. It was still warm enough to sit outside. Frank had succeeded in getting them a great table near the fountain. The mood was fun and festive. LaVerne told the waiter, the busboy, and anyone else within earshot that Linda was responsible for the new smash play that opened on Broadway last night.

Lunch ended and it was time to say good-bye again. The luggage had already been stored in the limo, and it would be taking the two couples to the airport where Frank's private plane was waiting to take them back to California.

Linda and Scott decided to take the ferry over to Ellis Island so Scott could get a close-up look at the Statue of Liberty.

On the way back from their sightseeing excursion, Scott and Linda had another talk.

"I thought of the perfect person to look at your play," Linda said, almost afraid to broach the subject again. Scott didn't comment, so she forged ahead. "Freddie Millhouse. He produced some of my earlier plays. He's a wonderful director."

"Ah, the man responsible for hooking you up with Hilary."

Linda was surprised that Scott remembered that. "Right."

Scott shrugged. "Whatever you say, honey. You're driving the tour bus. I'm just along for the ride."

Linda decided not to take Scott's comment to heart. She didn't want to argue. "I'm not sure where Freddie is at the moment, but Hilary will know."

The next day, Hilary and Linda had lunch with one of the producers from the Solomon Organization. Norman Tedesco was a tall bald man in his fifties. Linda thought he looked like Gary Cooper without hair. He had been around the theater quite a bit while they were working on *The Magic Camera,* but she didn't know him well.

Tedesco wanted to know if Linda had any other plays for them to read and consider for production.

"There's the one Dancer Productions bought the film rights to," Hilary said immediately. "It's a great play, and if the movie is well-received, you'll be guaranteed another hit."

"Does it have a musical score?"

"Not yet, but I think I can talk a certain composer into taking a look at it first."

"Great idea. Send a copy to my office by messenger," the producer said, nodding his bald head enthusiastically.

"I had a co-writer on the movie script," Linda heard herself saying. "Scott Richards. You met him at the opening. Anyway, he's very talented, and if the play needs to be rewritten to suit your needs, I'd like to bring him into the deal."

"Fine. Whatever you say, Linda. You're our shining star."

"Thank you." Linda sat quietly for the rest of the meal, eating her broiled fish. She felt a little giddy and had to squash the impulse to laugh out loud. Her life was spinning out of control, deliciously out of the realm of reality. She would not say a word to Scott about this right now. She needed time to build his confidence in himself and in the lifestyle she wanted to share with him.

After Tedesco left, Hilary patted her client's hand. "Pretty sly move, bringing Scott into the deal," she said.

"I'm desperate to keep him here, Hilary," Linda admitted.

"I don't blame you. He's worth hanging onto."

"He's written a new play on his own," Linda said. "I

want you to read it and then I want you to get it to Freddie. Tell him that I'll underwrite the production, if necessary."

"Is the play that bad?"

"No. It's actually wonderful. I just can't take too long finding a producer for it. And Freddie loves you; he'll do anything you say."

"Scott's ready to bolt on you?"

"He wants us both to go back to the beach. I can't do that now."

"Of course you can't. Besides, you two haven't known each other all that long, just a few months, actually. Take it from me, a long-term commitment shouldn't be entered into lightly. If there's the slightest doubt that you can make it work, you should definitely wait and see."

Linda laughed out loud. "Don't worry, Hilary. I'm not going to take off to California with Scott and make life difficult for you. I owe you a lot. I wouldn't be where I am today if it weren't for you."

Hilary sighed and sat back in her chair. "I'm sorry, but we just met with one of the biggest producers on Broadway. Your career is about to skyrocket. I'd have a breakdown if you left New York."

"Why does everything in life have to be so darn complicated?" Linda asked. "I don't want to jeopardize my career, but I don't want to lose Scott either.

"Where's that play he wrote? I'll call Freddie as soon as I get back to the office. I'll finance the production myself, if necessary."

Chapter Twenty-three

As it turned out, Freddie read the play and loved it. Scott and Linda had dinner with the off-Broadway producer the next week. He and Scott hit it off immediately.

"We need to start working on the production right away," Freddie told Scott. "The play we were going to mount next month didn't work out. The playwright never got it beyond the first act."

"Imagine that," Scott said with a twinkle in his blue eyes.

"Now my theater isn't Broadway. We can't pay you a ton of money, but I can guarantee that we will respect you and your work and stage a first-class production."

"Freddie is an excellent director. I learned so much from working with him," Linda told Scott.

"I took the liberty of bringing a contract with me, Scott. It's standard, approved by the Dramatists Guild."

"I'm not a member of the Dramatists Guild," Scott replied.

"It doesn't matter. Linda is, and she knows what the basic agreement is all about. It's okay if you want to take it with you and have Linda go over it with you."

"I'm sure it's fine," Scott said. "Where do I sign?"

Linda's hands were under the table, not visible to Scott or Freddie, so they couldn't see that the fingers on both of her hands were crossed.

"You do understand that as the playwright you will be taking an active part in the production?"

Scott nodded. "Linda promised to help out too."

"It's going to be great," Linda said, smiling first at Scott and then at Freddie. "Scott has been working in Hollywood on movie scripts. Writers don't get the respect there that playwrights receive here."

"That's why I work for my brother-in-law," Scott said. "He has to be nice to me or deal with my sister."

Freddie chuckled softly. "It all starts with the writing. Don't let anyone tell you different."

Scott signed the contract, and Linda's plan to keep him in New York was underway. Of course, that was only the beginning of Linda's plan. Keeping Scott in New York temporarily was one thing, making him like it and want to stay on permanently was something else entirely.

They had dined at a quaint little Italian restaurant in Linda's neighborhood. After dinner, Scott and Linda decided to walk back to her apartment.

"Are you happy now?" Scott asked, after Freddie left.

Linda was holding onto Scott's arm. She squeezed it and leaned her face against it. "Very."

"Good. That's why I signed the contract."

Linda straightened up and studied his face to see if he was joking. He wasn't. "Scott, I know that money and success aren't important to you." She sighed. "Sometimes I wish they weren't important to me, but they are."

Scott nodded. "I understand that."

"And that's why you're letting Freddie's theater produce your play? Just to make me happy?"

"Yes."

"Okay. I believe one of the reasons is to please me. I also believe you did it because you want your play to be staged. You want the validation only a live audience can give you. Come on. You can admit it."

Scott stopped walking and pulled Linda into his arms. "The only thing I'm admitting to is wanting to stay close to you, but I'm not going to let you keep me at arm's length much longer, Linda. Freddie said the play will open in a month. That's how much time you have to make up your mind. Then, we either commit to each other totally and merge our lives, or . . ."

Linda placed her fingers across his lips to silence him. "I don't want to hear the or," she said softly. "I want to make this work as much as you do, maybe more. You work on your play. Work on it honestly, no holding back. Experience the joy of seeing and hearing an audience respond to your story, your words. Then, we'll talk about a long-term commitment."

"Okay," Scott said. "I'll give it all I've got, for you, for us." This time there was no twinkle in his eye and no smile on his lips. His tone wasn't light and teasing; it was thoughtful and sober.

After Scott left, Linda stared out the window of her apartment. The sky was dark, the stars obscured by the industrial pollution of the city. *What am I doing to us?* she asked herself. *I've never been a manipulative person. I hate people like that, yet here I am trying to steer Scott into my lifestyle, hoping that he'll get caught up in it and want to stay in New York.*

Tears stung Linda's eyes. She wanted Scott, but she couldn't give up her dreams for him. The worst part was that Scott was fully aware of what she was trying to do. The fact that he was willing to go along with it, even temporarily, showed the depth of his feelings for her. Linda was risking their love on the hope that once Scott experienced the thrill of his own success, he would not be able to turn away from it. Or her.

Linda accompanied Scott to the theater the first day. Freddie's playhouse was around the corner and down three blocks from the Solomon, not too far off-Broadway. It was a small theater with a hundred seats. The stage, lights, and sound system were decent, and the actors and technical people who worked with Freddie were professionals.

Freddie Millhouse had begun his career as an actor. He

had a respectable acting resume, but directing was his true calling. He had moved from basement theaters, to off-off-Broadway houses, to his present location, where he and his wife of twenty-odd years had just recently set down roots.

Freddie and Catherine owned the old building sandwiched between a tailor shop and a bookstore, and lived upstairs from the theater. Catherine was the set designer and helped the actors with costumes. The Abigail Playhouse was named for their only child, a daughter who was married to a wealthy cattle rancher and lived in Texas. Linda suspected that Abigail and her husband were primary investors in the building and theater. New York real estate was very expensive.

Catherine was a redhead with spiked hair and a body that looked like a figure eight. She had a quick wit and a contagious laugh. The first time Linda had worked with Freddie and met his wife was shortly after her father's death. Catherine had recognized the lost look in the young playwright's eyes and took her under her wing. They'd been close friends ever since.

"So, when do we get tickets to your big Broadway hit?" Catherine asked, giving Linda a hug.

"I wanted you to come to the opening, but Freddie said you couldn't make it," Linda replied. "When do you want to go? I'll call the box office right now."

Catherine laughed. "Hilary sent us tickets. We're going tomorrow night. I hear she's got a new beau, the famous composer, no less."

"Right."

Scott, who had been whisked off by Freddie to inspect the backstage area, returned and Linda introduced him to Catherine.

"Nice to meet you," Scott said, shaking Catherine's hand.

"Well, aren't you a handsome rascal," Catherine replied.

"Thank you," Scott said, undaunted by her remark. "I owe it all to good genes. Wait till you meet my sister. She's really a knockout."

Catherine laughed and patted Scott on the shoulder. "You need anything, you just holler."

"Stop flirting with the playwright," Freddie said from the doorway. "He belongs to Linda."

"I know that," Catherine said. "Hilary gave me the scoop on everything."

He belongs to Linda. The words struck Linda in the pit of her stomach. She smiled to cover her sudden anxiety. Scott didn't belong to her at all. Scott belonged to the sun, the wind, the sand, and the ocean. Linda was trying to lasso the moon and pull it down to earth.

"Hey," Scott said. "Are you coming with us?"

Linda snapped out of her thoughts and smiled again. "Sure. Go on. I'll catch up." Scott and Freddie headed out the door that led onto the stage area. Linda turned to Catherine. "Do you have time to listen to the reading?" she asked.

"I've got some calls to make, then I'll slip into the theater. I haven't had a chance to look at Scott's script."

"It's a wonderful play," Linda told her. "You'll love it."

"Are you okay, honey?"

"Just nervous for Scott," Linda lied. She thought about confiding her real fears to Catherine and then decided against it. Talking about what she was trying to do and why would only make her guilt more palpable.

Linda took a seat in the theater. Freddie had an ensemble of actors that performed in most of his local productions. He had summoned six of them, four men and two women, to read through Scott's play.

A long table had been set up on the stage and copies of the script were already stacked on one end of it. As the actors entered, Freddie introduced Scott and instructed them to take a copy of the script and a seat at the table.

The plan was to have the actors read through the script aloud, while Freddie and Scott listened. Freddie assigned a part or parts to each actor.

"This is very preliminary," Freddie said when everyone

was organized. "You may not be cast in the part you're reading. You may not be cast in this play at all."

"We know how you work, Freddie," one of the male actors said blandly. "We won't get our hopes up."

"Okay. Before we start reading, Scott will give us a brief rundown on the storyline and the characters." Freddie nodded for Scott to begin.

Linda sat forward in her seat, waiting for Scott to speak. She felt like a mother hen pushing her chick out into the barnyard for the first time.

"The play is called *Lifelines*," Scott said. "It's about four men from different walks of life who are patients in the cancer ward of a veteran's hospital. Their paths would probably never cross outside the walls of this hospital ward, but here they are sharing a room and a life-threatening illness."

Linda let her breath out. Scott sounded confident and casual, as if he explained his storylines and characters on a regular basis.

"There are conflicts of course, and a love affair that began twenty years earlier is finally resolved," Scott said.

Linda continued to listen as Scott gave a brief description of each of the play's main characters. Catherine came into the theater and took a seat next to Linda.

Linda had intended to watch Catherine and monitor her reaction to the play, but once the actors began to read, Linda got so caught up in the story that she forgot all about Catherine.

Linda had already read the script, but these actors were seasoned professionals who brought the characters to life with skill and emotion.

"Lifelines," one of the actors said as the play ended. "Are the people we meet at crucial times in our lives, people who reach out and share our joys and our sorrows, people who sometimes change the course of our lives."

The words echoed through the empty theater. Linda nodded in agreement. Scott was her lifeline. Perhaps that was why she was trying so desperately to hang onto him.

Chapter Twenty-four

Lifelines was cast and in rehearsals within a few days. Scott spent all of his days and most of his nights at the theater. Linda had planned on being there to help out, but with the success of *The Magic Camera*, Linda's post-production schedule had become all the more busy and de-manding.

Scott and Linda's private moments became few and far between, but Scott seemed to be enjoying the production process and didn't complain about all the work he was do-ing.

Towards the end of the month, each time Linda saw Scott, she felt a pang of guilt. Scott's carefree attitude seemed to be buried under a serious concern for Freddie and Catherine and their financial future.

"They are putting so much into this production," Scott told Linda. "If it bombs, they'll lose a bundle."

"It's not going to bomb," Linda assured him. "Freddie's reputation in this town is golden because he has a sixth sense when it comes to choosing good plays and talented playwrights."

"Except in my case, where he was influenced by his af-fection for you and Hilary."

Linda drew in a sharp breath. "Yes, he was initially. He probably wouldn't have considered your play otherwise, but Freddie is no pushover. He decided to produce the play based on its own merits and your talent."

Scott nodded without smiling. Lately, Scott's dazzling smile had been hiding, like the sun on a cloudy day. There were times when Linda ached to see Scott's impetuous grin and recapture those magical days at the beach when all they thought about was having fun and falling in love.

Seeing the changes in Scott often made Linda regret her stubborn resolve to push his career forward. Scott had come to New York to support her. He had stayed in New York and committed to this production to please her.

It was said that absence made the heart grow fonder. Being deprived of Scott's time and attention was making Linda want him all the more. Her ambition and success had built a wall between them. Linda could only hope that their love was strong enough to tear it down when Scott's play opened and the time limit he had set for them expired.

Scott's play was set to preview on a Thursday night. The audience was to be a select group, a mixture of media people and friends.

Carla flew in that morning on a commercial flight because Frank was in London negotiating a deal for the foreign rights to one of his films.

Carla arrived at the condo in a limousine. Linda was there to meet her and take her to lunch because Scott was doing an interview for a local television station.

"Scott is being interviewed?" Carla asked with disbelief in her voice. "This is a first."

"He's been working so hard on this production," Linda told her. "He's almost a different person."

Carla stopped unpacking her small suitcase and looked at Linda curiously. "I'm amazed," she admitted. "I guess the power of love is stronger than I thought possible."

Linda felt the color rise to her cheeks. "To be honest, I've been feeling guilty for pushing him so hard."

"Don't be ridiculous," Carla replied. "Scott needed a good push. I'm delighted that you've gotten him to do something positive with his talent. Up till now, all he's done is rewrite other people's work, and getting him to do that was harder than convincing a small child to eat vegetables instead of ice cream. My husband is the only producer in Hollywood who is willing to give Scott assignments."

"He's so talented," Linda told her. "Wait until you see his play tonight. It really is wonderful."

"I think working with you on your script made all the difference. Frank was afraid when you left, Scott would go back to his old tricks and hold up production on the film. Scott surprised us all with his dedication to the project. Of course, Scott's feelings for you were the true motivation behind his new stability."

Linda lowered herself into the nearest chair. "That's just it, Carla. Ever since I met Scott I've been prodding him to write more and to work harder. Now I'm afraid I may have gone too far. As I said before, he's almost a different person."

"Good. Scott's been a kid far too long. It's time he grew up."

Linda forced a smile. "Where would you like to go for lunch?"

"How about the Carnegie Deli? I'm dying for some New York cheesecake."

One of the benefits of her newfound success was the priority treatment Linda received at restaurants in the theater district. The Carnegie Deli was mobbed, but Linda and Carla were immediately seated and served.

After lunch, Carla wanted to go shopping. "I brought a dress for tonight, but I want a new one for the actual opening tomorrow night."

Linda and Carla spent the afternoon shopping, and, by the time she got back to her own apartment, Linda's feet were aching. She called the theater and asked for Scott, but Catherine answered and told her she had sent everyone home to unwind before the evening's performance.

Linda called the condo, but Carla said Scott hadn't

showed up there yet. "Do you want him to call you when
he gets here?" she asked.

"No. I'll see him at the theater. I'm going early in case
Freddie or Catherine need help with something."

"Okay. I'll see you there," Carla said cheerfully. "I've
got to go and soak my feet so they'll fit in the new shoes
I bought today."

Linda laughed and hung up the phone. She needed to
soak her feet as well, and headed for the tub and her bath
salts.

Linda dressed conservatively and arrived at the Abigail
Playhouse an hour before curtain time. She intended to stay
in the background and avoid the media. This was Scott's
night and she was only there to support him.

Nominations for the Tony Awards were to be announced
at the end of next week. *The Magic Camera* was sure to
garner some nominations, and Linda would be besieged
with media attention again. However, Linda was deter-
mined not to let her public image overshadow Scott's first
professional production.

"Where's Scott?" Linda asked Catherine when she
slipped in the back door of the theater.

"That's what everyone wants to know," Catherine replied. "I told him to unwind, not disappear."

"His sister arrived this afternoon. They're probably just
catching up and running a little late. What can I do to
help?"

"Fold these programs. The printer just delivered them.
They were supposed to fold them but claim their machine
broke down. Just do a hundred and take them out to the
lobby, please."

Linda grabbed a stack of programs and began folding
them quickly and deftly. Catherine ran off to finish dressing. Freddie's booming voice could be heard backstage issuing instructions to the stage crew.

Linda's cell phone rang.

Scott was on the other end of the phone. "Hi, sugar.
Where are you?"

"I'm at the theater folding programs. Where are you?"

"At the top of the Empire State Building."

"What are you doing there?" Linda asked with panic in her voice.

"Looking at the view. All these weeks I've been in New York and I've never seen it at night. It's really awesome."

"Where's Carla?"

"I sent her on ahead."

"Scott," Linda said slowly, controlling the impulse to raise her voice. "You need to get over here right away."

"Why don't you come here instead?"

"What?"

"Jump in a cab and meet me on top of the Empire State Building."

"You're crazy."

"Maybe, but work on the play is done. Your time is up. And all the romantic films shot in New York have the guy and girl meeting on the top of the Empire State Building. They rush into each other's arms and shut out the rest of the world. I'll stand by the elevator with my arms open. How soon can you get here?"

"Catherine told me to fold the programs and bring them to the lobby. The programs are for your play. You remember that, don't you?"

"Oh, is that tonight?"

"Scott, please stop fooling around and get over here," Linda said, her voice rising in increased panic.

"Okay."

The phone clicked off. "Scott? Scott?"

"What?" his voice came from behind her. Linda spun around to see him standing in the doorway, holding up Carla's cell phone. "These things are actually a lot of fun," he said.

"I'm going to kill you," Linda said.

"Before or after tonight's performance?" The old grin was back, lighting up the room. He crossed over to her and pulled her into his arms. "If you really loved me, you would have run out the door and flagged down a cab."

"If I didn't love you, I wouldn't be standing here folding these programs," Linda countered.

"Will you meet me on top of the Empire State building after the show?"

"It'll be closed for the night."

"Better yet. We can be completely alone. Something that hasn't happened much the last month or so." Scott kissed her and held her close. Linda reveled in the feel of his body against hers.

"Hey," Freddie shouted, bounding into the room. "Cut out the mush and get out there and meet your public, Scott. Linda, give me those programs. There's none in the lobby."

Scott and Linda pulled apart. Linda handed Freddie the programs she had already folded. "I'll be out with the rest in a few minutes," she promised.

"Good girl."

Freddie took Scott by the arm and escorted him out of the office. Linda hurriedly finished her job and rushed out to deliver the rest of the programs.

People were streaming into the theater. Freddie was introducing Scott to everyone who passed by. Scott seemed perfectly relaxed.

Linda left the lobby and found her seat in the back of the theater next to Carla. "Your brother is nuts," she whispered.

"Always has been," Carla agreed. "Where is he now?"

"In the lobby with Freddie. He seems perfectly at ease. I don't understand how he can be so calm."

"I asked him that on the way over here. He said he'd done his best and now it was out of his hands, so there was no point in worrying."

Linda sighed. "He's right, I guess. Besides, I'm nervous enough for both of us."

The media people were always the last to arrive. They began to arrive ten minutes before curtain time and made their way down the center aisle to the seats that had been reserved for them in the front rows.

Scott slid into the seat next to Linda and took hold of

her hand. The lights flashed and then dimmed. The curtain rose and the stage lights came up on the set that Catherine and her crew had designed.

It looked just like an actual hospital ward, and Linda squeezed Scott's hand to let him know she was impressed with the set where all the action would take place.

The preview performance was not perfect. Actors dropped lines, and a phone rang after the actor had already picked it up, but the audience didn't seem to notice or mind. They were too caught up in the story and characters Scott had created.

When the play ended the applause was loud and enthusiastic, and Scott was escorted on stage to take a bow.

Linda and Carla hugged each other and cried for joy. Scott's smile was brighter than the stage lights, and after the show he was surrounded by reporters, especially female reporters.

As she had planned, Linda stayed in the background for the rest of the weekend, letting Scott have his time in the limelight.

An off-Broadway show didn't get the immediate front-page media coverage that a Broadway show garnered. The reviews trickled into the papers and onto the radio airwaves over the next week. Most were very favorable. The opening weekend had been sold-out and Freddie reported that the play was selling out for the rest of its run and he wanted to extend it another few weeks.

Linda was ecstatic. Scott seemed to take it all in stride.

On Monday, Carla went back to California and Linda thought she and Scott would find some quiet time to discuss their future together, but the Solomon Organization had other plans for Linda's time.

The press was leaking the news that *The Magic Camera* had scored a record number of Tony nominations and the media frenzy began even though no one on the Tony nominating committee would confirm or deny the rumors.

The Solomon Organization took advantage of the new buzz by sponsoring a different event each night with Ken and Linda as featured guests. The events were meant to attract new investors for future shows, and they showed up in droves to be wined and dined and impressed by Ken and Linda's successful show.

"I'll bet those rumors that leaked were actually planted by Solomon's publicity people," Linda told Ken as they left the last scheduled event of the week.

"Well, we'll know tomorrow morning if they're true," Ken replied. "Then we'll have a few more days of craziness, and then it will die down until the week before the awards ceremony."

"I hope so," Linda said. "I've barely seen Scott this week. How are you and Hilary doing?"

"Hasn't she told you?"

"We haven't had time to talk about anything but business this week. What's going on?"

"Our kids hate each other, so we've decided to cool it for awhile."

"Oh, Ken, I'm so sorry."

"So am I. Actually, I've been pretty miserable without her, and I'm hoping she's suffering too."

Linda laughed. "So the separation may bring you closer."

"Something like that."

"Well, Scott and I don't have kids to keep us apart, but our individual successes are doing a pretty good job of keeping us in separate corners."

Linda knew that her preoccupation with the Solomon Organization this past week had taken a toll on her relationship with Scott.

She also knew that Freddie had been pressuring Scott to talk to a producer he knew who might take Scott's play to Broadway. Catherine had told Hilary, and Hilary had told Linda. Scott hadn't told Linda himself, and that in itself worried her.

Linda decided to call Scott as soon as she got home. It was late, but she wanted to hear his voice. Better yet, she would have the Solomon's driver drop her off at the condo. She and Scott needed to have a face-to-face discussion.

She wanted to melt into Scott's arms and have him tell her he understood why she was away from him. She wanted to talk to him about his own success. She wanted to tell him how much she loved him.

Chapter Twenty-five

The driver dropped Ken off at his apartment and Linda then asked the driver to take her to the Dancers' condo.

The driver complied with Linda's request, but then insisted on waiting in case the person she was going to see wasn't at home.

"No. I'm sure he'll be there," Linda said. "Besides, I have my cell phone. If he's not there, I'll call a cab."

"Please, miss," the driver said. "I'm responsible for getting you home safely. Mr. Tedesco will have my hide if there's any mix-up."

Linda smiled at him. "All right. I'll call Scott and make sure he's there so you can leave me here without worrying."

Linda punched in the phone number on her cell phone. The number rang and rang and rang. She hung up and tried again; still the phone didn't answer.

"Well," Linda said, forcing a smile. "I guess you were right to wait. You can take me home now."

The driver started the car and delivered Linda to her door within ten minutes. He walked her inside the building and made sure she got into her apartment.

Linda thanked him and closed her door and locked it.

She told herself that Scott must have unplugged the

phone, or he was sleeping so soundly he didn't hear it ringing.

Linda dumped her purse and coat on a chair in the living room. She picked up the phone and dialed the number for her answering service. She had several messages, but none of them were from Scott. She suddenly realized how exhausted she was.

"As Scarlett O'Hara would say, 'Tomorrow is another day,'" Linda said to a framed photo of her and Scott that Charlie and LaVerne had sent her. It was taken the night of the luau. They were dressed in their Hawaiian outfits and looked as relaxed and happy as two people could look.

Linda shook her head and sighed. Tomorrow was another day, and she would tell Scott how much she loved him. She would tell him that if he wanted to return to the beach after the Tony Awards, she would go with him.

Even if *The Magic Camera* didn't get all the predicted nominations, it would be extremely bad form not to attend the awards ceremony. Scott would understand that. Perhaps Scott would tell her that *Lifelines* was going to Broadway and he wanted to stay in New York. After all that had happened to her this year, anything was possible.

Hanging onto that happy thought allowed Linda to fall into a deep, dreamless sleep. She awoke to the ringing of her telephone. Sunlight was streaming into her windows as Linda groped for the phone and spoke huskily into the mouthpiece.

"Linda," Hilary screamed. "Where are you? I thought you were coming here to wait for the announcement."

"I'm sorry. I forgot to set the alarm. What time is it?"

"It's time you started working on that acceptance speech," Hilary shouted. "*The Magic Camera* has been nominated in almost every category."

Linda was instantly awake. "I got nominated for the book?"

"Of course you got nominated for writing the book! The script was great even before Ken put music to it."

"What about the actors?"

"Lead actors and supporting actors; Rick will be insufferable if he wins."

"I think I'm going to cry," Linda whispered.

"I already did that. I couldn't be happier for you and Ken," Hilary said with a catch in her voice. "Now get yourself together and get over here."

Linda hung up and immediately dialed the number at the condo. Once again, the phone rang and went unanswered. Since the Dancers didn't spend a lot of time there, they didn't have an answering service or machine on that phone.

Linda hung up the telephone and it rang. She snatched it up again. "Hello."

"How's the most gorgeous and talented woman in New York city?"

"Rick. Congratulations on your nomination," Linda said, disappointed that it was him instead of Scott.

"Congratulations on yours, darling. How about having lunch with me to celebrate our good fortune?"

"Sorry. Can't do it today. Hilary is expecting me at her office. I'm already late."

"Okay, but I insist on a rain check."

"Sure."

Linda ended the phone call and dashed for the bathroom. She showered and shampooed and styled her hair in record time. She would hail a taxi to take her to Hillary's office, and, on the way, she would stop by the condo and see Scott. She was still clinging to the thought that he had unplugged the phone.

Linda was reaching for the door handle when the bell rang. She opened the door to find a messenger with a small vase of yellow roses.

She signed for the flowers and carried them over to a table in the living room. An envelope was attached to the flowers. She opened it and took out a note.

"Dear Linda, Congratulations on the Tony nominations you are sure to receive. By the time you get this message, I will be back at the beach. Forgive me for running out on you and not saying a proper good-bye. I have come to realize that everything you need and want is in New York. I can't ask you to give it up and I can't stay. Be happy and enjoy your success. Love, Scott."

Linda read the note over and over again. Her telephone rang constantly, but she didn't answer it.

The words on the note cut through her, piercing her heart and ravaging her soul. Scott was gone and he wasn't coming back. He had given up on her and their love.

Her attempts to keep him in New York had failed. It was her fault that Scott was now turning his back on all that they had, on all that they could have had together.

Linda was too stunned to cry, too hurt to scream. She sat there for a long time, clutching the note and staring at the flowers.

Finally, the doorbell rang again. Linda rose to her feet and walked to the door. Another delivery man with another vase of flowers, this one so enormous the man could hardly hold onto it.

"Put them on the kitchen counter," Linda said woodenly. "And please take those yellow roses on the table. Deliver them to a nursing home or hospital."

"Seriously?" the delivery man asked.

"Yes, please," Linda replied. She opened her purse, took out a generous tip, and held it out to him.

"Whatever you say, lady," the man said, picking up Scott's flowers and heading out the door.

Linda walked over and read the note attached to the larger floral arrangement. It was from the Solomon Organization, congratulating her on the Tony nominations.

Then, she pick up her coat and purse and left the apartment, locking the door behind her.

Later that day, Linda stopped at the Abigail Playhouse and talked to Freddie and Catherine.

"I didn't know he was leaving," Freddie told Linda. "But Catherine did."

"He had that lost-puppy look all week," Catherine said. "He said we could run *Lifelines* as long as we wanted, but he didn't want to take it to Broadway. I tried to call you, to get you to talk to him for Freddie's sake, but you didn't call me back."

"No. I didn't," Linda said. "I was too busy to call you back or talk to Scott. I thought I would catch up on everything after the nominations were announced. They tell me things will quiet down for awhile now."

"*Lifelines* is selling out every weekend," Freddie said. "We'll keep it running for awhile. Maybe Scott will change his mind and come back."

"I don't think so," Linda said. "He told me all along that he didn't want to stay here, that he would end up disappointing me, but I didn't want to believe it."

"You'll be going back to California for your movie premiere in a few months. You'll see Scott then and work it out with him."

Linda shook her head. "I don't know if that's possible, Freddie. The Solomon Organization wants to do a musical based on the same script Dancer bought the film rights to. I've got to stay here and work on that with Ken. I *want* to stay here and work on it." Tears started forming in her eyes.

"Of course you do," Freddie said with forced cheerfulness. "These opportunities don't come along every day. You've got to grab the gold ring and hang onto it."

"You're right," Linda said. "I guess."

Chapter Twenty-six

The weeks leading up to the Tony Awards ceremony were long and lonely. Hilary was negotiating the new contract with the Solomon Organization, but Ken and Linda decided not to do any work on the script or music until everything was finalized.

There were plenty of other offers on the table for Linda, but she didn't want to commit to anything else right now. She was tired physically and drained emotionally.

Rick Ralston called every day and sent flowers on a regular basis, but Linda refused to start dating him again. As the lead actor in her hit Broadway show, it was impossible to avoid him completely. Whenever they met, Rick acted like they were a couple, and Linda's coolness towards him did little to discourage him.

"He's knocking himself out to win you back," Hilary told her over lunch one day. "You could do worse."

"He's giving my ego a much needed boost," Linda admitted. "But it won't last."

"You could be wrong," Hilary said.

"I could be," Linda replied. "And cows could start grazing in Central Park."

Hilary laughed. "How's the new play coming?"

"It's about finished, but I don't think it's very good."

"Linda, you could write about the cows grazing in Central Park and it would sell tomorrow. You're one hot property."

"For the moment."

"Have you heard from Scott?"

"Not a word."

"Sorry."

"So am I. I talked to LaVerne yesterday. She said Scott isn't talking to anyone right now, not even her and Charlie."

"I think we'd better change the subject," Hilary decided. "What are you wearing to the awards ceremony?"

"I don't know. What are you wearing?"

"I don't know. I think we'd better finish lunch and go do some serious shopping."

On the night of the awards, The Solomon Organization once again provided Linda with a limousine and driver. Linda recognized the driver as the same man who had driven her to the Dancers' condo a few weeks earlier. Linda acknowledged him with a smile as he helped her into the back of the car.

Although Linda arrived at the Tony Awards ceremony unescorted, Rick Ralston deftly managed to make it appear like they were together. He slipped out of the crowd at the front of the theater and took her arm as soon as she alighted from the car, as if their meeting were prearranged.

Linda was dressed in a long dress of pale green velvet with a plain jeweled neckline and long sleeves. A simple strand of pearls with matching earrings completed the outfit.

"You look divine, darling," Rick said.

Rick's lean, tall physique was made for a tuxedo, and he looked heartbreakingly handsome, but Linda couldn't help but think how much happier she would be with Scott at her side.

Rick and Linda were escorted into the theater by security people, but did stop a few times to pose for photographers.

Rick's efforts over the past few weeks to win Linda back

had resulted in rumors of their romance being run in all the New York gossip columns. Linda wondered if the rumors would make the California papers. Scott never bothered reading the newspapers, but it was possible someone would relate the stories to him.

Linda shook her head to clear it. Thoughts of Scott had to be banished, especially tonight. They lived in separate, conflicting worlds—wanted different things from life—and perhaps it was time she accepted the fact that they might never be able to resolve those differences.

"Smile, darling," Rick whispered, as they were ushered to their seats in the front of the theater. "Everyone is looking at us."

Linda snapped to attention and smiled. She had an obligation to the Solomon Organization and to herself to present a good, positive image tonight. "Thanks for reminding me," she said sincerely.

Although the consensus was that *The Magic Camera* would win every award it was nominated for, it didn't work out that way. The redheaded girl with perfect pitch won in the best supporting actress category, but in the other categories in which *The Magic Camera* actors were nominated the Tonys went to other actors.

Rick Ralston lost out to a lead actor in a straight drama and Linda could tell he was bitterly disappointed. The last awards to be announced were for Best Musical Score, Best Book for a Musical, and overall Best New Play. *The Magic Camera* won all three.

Linda's acceptance speech was short and emotional. She thanked everyone involved with the production and said she was accepting the award on behalf of her late father, who had originated the story for the script.

The Solomon Organization held a gala celebration after the awards show. Rick was excellent in his role as a gracious loser. It wasn't until he and Linda were in the car on the way to her apartment that he became irritable and distant.

"It was your first nomination," Linda told him. "There will be many more opportunities for you."

"I need some tender loving care," he said, reaching out for her.

He tried to draw Linda into his arms, but she pulled away from him. She was sorry she had agreed to let him escort her home.

"Another rejection," he said sarcastically. "Just what I needed tonight. Thanks a lot, Linda."

"I'm sorry, Rick," Linda replied evenly. "But I'm not ready to get involved with you or anyone else right now."

"Still carrying a torch for the beach boy?" Linda turned away from him. "Of course you are. Well, get over it, darling. The guy's a loser. You want to stay on top in this town, you've got to be seen with the right people."

Linda wanted to remind him that he was the biggest loser she had seen that night, but decided not to waste her time provoking him further.

By the time they got to Linda's door, Rick was charmingly contrite. "I apologize for my bad behavior. Say you forgive me."

"I forgive you, Rick. I know it's been a disappointing night for you."

"I'll make it up to you, I promise. I was a fool to ever let you slip away from me. I want you to trust me, Linda. I want you to love me."

"Good night, Rick," Linda said pointedly, as she pushed her door open and slipped inside the apartment.

"I'll call you tomorrow," Rick called out as she shut the door firmly in his handsome face.

Alone in her apartment, Linda sat in a chair facing the window and looked at the award she had coveted for so long. It was a beautiful prize, a shining symbol of all that she had achieved over the past year.

Linda thought about all the years of struggling that had led to that moment when her name was announced tonight. Not only had she reached all the lofty goals she had set for herself, she had somehow managed to surpass them.

She pressed the beautiful trophy to her chest as the tears slid silently down her face. At that moment, she would have gladly traded the prestigious Tony Award for the warmth and comfort of Scott's arms.

Chapter Twenty-seven

The next morning, LaVerne and Charlie called to congratulate her.

"Your picture's on the front page of the *LA Times* with tall, dark, and handsome. You two getting together again?" LaVerne asked.

"No. It's strictly a publicity shot. How are things at the beach?"

"Sorry, honey. I haven't seen him at all. Charlie went down there this morning and left a copy of the newspaper on his back step."

"Why did he do that?"

"'Cause Charlie thinks Scott is being a horse's you-know-what. I guess Scott knows it too. That's why he's been holed up in the house all this time avoiding everyone."

Then, Charlie got on the phone. "Hey, cutie, you coming back here for the movie premiere? It's your big chance to see yours truly steal that picture you wrote."

Linda laughed. "I don't know what my schedule is going to be."

"Doesn't matter. I'll tell Frank to send his private plane for you. Whisk you back and forth in the same day. Surely you can spare a day for your old friends?"

"Of course I can," Linda promised. "I'll see you then."

A few minutes later, Carla and Frank called to congratulate her. "I'm taking the newspaper out to the beach house to show Scott," Carla said firmly.

"I think Charlie already left him a copy."

"Well, he's going to get a second copy and a lecture from his big sister. He should have been in the photo with you."

"Please, Carla, don't push it. It wasn't Scott's fault. I tried to manipulate him and force success down his throat. It was wrong, and Scott had good reason to break it off with me."

"Do you really feel that way?" Carla asked.

"Yes. I really do. I think it's all for the best for both of us." Linda didn't really feel that way at all, but she didn't want to cause trouble between Scott and his sister. Then, to change the subject, she told Carla about the Solomon Organization wanting to produce a stage musical of *The Last Laugh*.

Carla screamed and put Frank on the phone to hear it for himself. "That's terrific, Linda. I'd better hurry up and get that picture released. I'll call you with a definite date in a few weeks and I'll even send my plane to New York to get you."

"Thanks. That's very nice of you."

As much as Linda wanted to attend the premiere of *The Last Laugh*, she wasn't sure she could handle seeing Scott again. Her feelings for him were still strong, and her regrets over the way she had tried to control him were even stronger.

Fortunately, the contract negotiations for the Broadway staging of *The Last Laugh* were concluded that same morning. That meant that Ken and Linda could now start work on the music and the script.

Ken admitted that he already had a few tunes in mind, and he and Linda began their collaboration. The work was wonderful therapy, and Linda threw herself into the project with all her energy.

Ken and Hilary had decided to ignore their children's protests and were seeing each other on a regular basis again. After working on the script all day, Linda usually joined them for dinner before going home to her apartment. She continued to concentrate on her work, but thoughts of Scott were constantly intruding, causing her to relive all the mistakes she had made in their relationship.

The new musical project was going well, and Freddie wanted to produce one of Linda's old plays at the Abigail Playhouse.

"I know you're busy with your new project," Freddie told her the day he phoned. "Just come by and give me your input on the casting, and I'll do the rest."

"I didn't think you still remembered that old script," Linda said.

"Honey, you're a star now. Take out all those old scripts you've got stored in the closet and have Hilary send them around. I guarantee theaters will be begging to produce them."

"Even the bad ones?" Linda asked.

"You couldn't write a bad one if you tried," Freddie said. "You're the golden girl."

Linda hung up with the praise ringing in her ears. *I'm golden all right,* Linda thought. *The money and offers are pouring in. Everything I ever wanted is mine, and yet none of it matters without Scott.*

Hilary had been bugging Linda to move uptown to a better address. Maybe it was time she did just that. Rehearsals for *The Last Laugh* wouldn't be starting for a few months. Solomon didn't want to compete with *The Magic Camera* too soon.

It didn't take Linda long to find a nice apartment facing Central Park. Within a few weeks, she was moved in.

"It's a fresh start," she told Hilary.

"I think you should throw a party. Let everyone see your new digs."

"Okay," Linda agreed. "I'll do it."

It was while the party was in full swing that the call came in from Dancer Productions. There was so much noise in the apartment, Linda could barely hear the information Julie was giving her.

"The premiere is next Saturday," Julie shouted into the phone. "Frank wants you to fly in Friday morning. He'll send his plane for you."

"Okay," Linda heard herself shout back. "Just let me know what time and I'll be at the airport."

Julie hung up, but Linda continued holding the phone in her hand. She hadn't been able to ask the one question that burned in her mind. Was Scott going to be there?

The thought of seeing him again filled Linda with a mixture of joy and dread.

Rick Ralston approached, took the phone from her hand, and hung it up. "Bad news?" he asked with concern in his dark eyes.

"No."

"Good. Come sit with me."

Rick put a possessive arm around her waist, and Linda let him lead her over to one of her brand-new elegant sofas. Linda had invited the entire cast of *The Magic Camera* to the party, but Rick seemed to think it was her way of making up to him.

Rick was talking nonstop, filling her in on all his exciting escapades over the past month or so. Linda barely heard a word he said. All she could think about was the possibility of seeing Scott again. What would she say? What would he say? Would she be able to keep herself from begging Scott to love her again?

When the plane touched down on the airstrip at Los Angeles International Airport reserved for private planes, Linda gazed out the window.

It was February and the sun was shining. The pilot had announced that the temperature was seventy-four degrees. The temperature in New York when she left a few hours earlier had been in the thirties.

She had expected Frank to send one of his assistants to

pick her up; instead she found Carla standing in the sun waiting for her.

They embraced. In casual slacks and a loose-fitting blouse, Carla looked as relaxed and beautiful as ever.

Linda was dressed all wrong for the warm day, in wool slacks and a sweater.

"I didn't realize it would be this warm," Linda said after she slipped into the car.

"No matter. We can stop and buy you some new clothes if you like. We'll charge them to Frank."

Linda laughed. "No, thanks. Frank has done enough for me. I have some lighter-weight clothes in my suitcase."

"It's a lot cooler at the beach," Carla said, keeping her eyes on the road leading out of the airport.

"I'm not going to the beach."

"I wish you would."

"Why?"

Carla suddenly pulled off the road and stopped the car. "Listen, Linda, I hate to burden you with this, but I'm really worried about Scott. He's been sequestered in that beach house ever since he came back from New York. He won't talk to me, or Frank, or even LaVerne or Charlie. He shut himself away from the world. When I went out there the other day to tell him about the premiere, he told me he wasn't going to any more of our phoney fiascos."

"Carla, you know Scott hates all the glitz and glamour. I'm not surprised."

"I know, but it's more than that. Scott has locked himself away and I'm really concerned about him. I was hoping maybe you'd drive out to the beach and try to talk to him."

"I don't know, Carla."

"Please, Linda. I think you're the only one he might listen to."

"I may be the last one he would listen to."

"But could you try, please? I'd consider it a huge personal favor and so would Frank."

Linda bit her lip. She had been hoping to meet Scott casually at the premiere. If he turned his back on her, she would have a crowd of people to get lost in. A face-to-face confrontation at the beach house terrified her, but after all the Dancers had done for her, it seemed selfish to refuse to talk to Scott on their behalf.

"Okay. I'll try, but he may not talk to me either."

Carla smiled and reached out and squeezed Linda's hand. "Thank you. You can drop me at Frank's office and use my car."

"Now?"

"The premiere is tomorrow. You have to talk to him today."

After dropping Carla at Dancer Productions, Linda headed out to the beach. As she drove, she began to rehearse what she would say to Scott. As she rehearsed, she began to feel more and more off-balance. By the time she arrived at the beach house, she was more nervous than she'd been before her Broadway debut.

Linda parked the car, got out, and slammed the door. She pounded up the stairs as fast as she could, afraid that if she hesitated she would lose her nerve and run. She was about to bang on the door when Scott opened it.

"Hey," he said with one of his high-voltage smiles. "What are you doing here?"

"I came to talk to you," Linda said. "Can I come in?"

"Sure."

Scott stepped aside and Linda hurried through the door. He was dressed in a pair of jeans with a plaid flannel shirt hanging loose around his hips. His blond hair was longer than usual and curled around the back of his shirt collar. His face was clean shaven, and his eyes were as clear and blue as the sky on a bright summer day.

The house was a mess and Linda stepped over the debris and made her way to the wall of windows that faced the ocean. When she got there she turned around and faced Scott.

"Carla asked me to come out here and talk to you," Linda began evenly. "I didn't know if you'd want to see me, but

Carla's really worried about you, so I said I'd try to talk to you."

"You look so good," Scott said, moving closer and smiling at her again. "I told Carla I didn't want to go to the premiere, but if you ask me . . ."

Linda was suddenly angry at him and the situation she was in. "I didn't come out here to ask you for a date, Scott. I came out here to tell you that turning your back on me is one thing, but turning your back on your family is something else entirely. I know I was wrong to try and manipulate you, but what you're doing now is just as bad. You have talent that you could be using to make the world a better, happier place. If you don't want to do that, fine. That's your choice to make, but you shouldn't be cutting yourself off from the world and your family. It's wrong, Scott, and you know it's wrong and . . ."

Just then a telephone rang. Linda stopped. Her cell phone was in the car in her purse. The phone continued to ring.

"Excuse me," Scott said. Linda watched in amazement as Scott walked over to the desk and answered a phone that was buried under a stack of papers. "Scott Richards. Oh yes, Mr. Denton, I got the contract for the film rights, but I think it may be a little premature. My novel isn't scheduled for release until the middle of the year."

"Your novel?" Linda whispered. "What novel?"

As Scott continued to talk to Mr. Denton, Linda moved over to the desk and began sorting through the junk. Under an empty cola can she found a manuscript titled *Lifelines.* Scott had written a novel based on his play. She turned over the title page and saw that the next page was the dedication page.

"To Linda, who opened the door to my mind and new possibilities with her faith in me, and kept it from slamming shut again with her love."

Tears clouded Linda's vision as she turned to the next page and began to read the opening paragraphs of the novel.

Scott ended his phone call and stood up. "That's what

I've been doing the last few months. I sent the proposal to an agent and he sold it in three days. The fact that the play had been produced in New York really helped. Anyway, once it sold, I had to finish the book. That's why I've been holed up here. You know how hard it is for me to concentrate."

"And you got a telephone?"

"Just a few days ago, after I sent the manuscript off. I was going to use it to call you, but I guess it's too late for that."

"You dedicated your book to me."

"Sure, who else? You're the first and only person who ever really believed in me."

"Lots of people believe in you, Scott."

Scott shrugged. "So I hear you won that big award. Congratulations. I saw your picture in the paper with Ralston. I know it's petty, but I'm really glad he didn't win. Bad enough he got the girl."

"He didn't get the girl, at least not this girl," Linda said softly. "She's in love with someone else."

"Anyone I know?"

"Yes. He just sold his first novel, and he has a new telephone."

Scott closed the distance between them in one long stride. He gathered Linda into his arms and kissed her lips, her face, her hair, her eyes. "I've missed you so much," he whispered. "I couldn't say good-bye in person or I would never have been able to leave you. And I had to leave. I had to prove that I could succeed on my own."

"Oh, Scott, none of that matters anymore. I have awards and piles of money, and it's all meaningless without you."

Scott pulled back and grinned at her. "Are you offering to support me again?"

"No. You don't need my support."

"But I need you. I love you."

"I love you," Linda said, melting against him.

The telephone rang again. "See why I hate these things?" Scott asked. He pulled her around the front of the desk and picked up the phone. "Scott Richards. Yes, actually my co-writer on the film is here with me now." He put the receiver against his chest. "Some reporter from *Variety*. Wants to know if we're going to work on another project together."

"You bet we are," Linda said, drawing closer to him.

Scott spoke into the phone again. "We're working on a love story," he said with a smile in his voice. "And I guarantee it will have a happy ending."

Epilogue

Scott and Linda were married within a few weeks. Scott's novel was an instant bestseller and then a major motion picture. He became as successful in his own right as Linda was in hers. Scott now worked more and played less while Linda now played more and worked less. After a year of traveling back and forth between coasts, Scott and Linda decided that the beach house would be their second home. They purchased a charming, spacious house in Connecticut as their new primary residence. It was a reasonable commute to New York, making Linda happy and a short walk to a beach, making Scott happy. The house was located in a small, friendly community, an ideal place to raise a family . . . and continue writing together.